The Adven...res
of
Vik the Vole

By Huw Williams

TO GRACE HOPE YOU
ENJOY THIS bOOK

Huw Will X

Thanks to

Neil Wyatt

Jeremy Wyatt

for their help.

One: The Cousins Rodent

Half out of control, he raced forward. Flat out, full tilt, pell-mell. He flashed a terrified, excited look over his shoulder. His pursuer was closing, his sharp teeth bared, plunging after him, straining, gaining. He twisted left, then right as he tore through the leaf litter. He saw it too late. Frantically, he tried to halt. *Stromp* – he jarred heavily against a fallen acorn, hurting his shoulder in the process. He had lost a few vital feet, but a few seconds later it was his tormentor's turn to slam against the acorn, howling a painful shriek. Vik knew his advantage was restored.

Up a muddy incline now, his lungs straining to suck in air, his heart beating so furiously it felt as if it would leap from his body. He reached the brow of a small hill and, without stopping, he powered his way over it and down, the leaves all around him crackling with their Autumn dryness. His downhill momentum was pulling him away from the creature, bigger and more powerful than he, his agility telling as he extracted those few vital metres. Nearly safe, almost home.

Another look over his shoulder, more confident now as he reached the bottom of the hill, saw his attacker fading. With a half grin he turned to face front. *Splutt* – he cartwheeled through the air to land heavily on his back, though the carpet of leaves had taken some of the force out of his fall. Everything had gone black. He tried to open his eyes, but they disobeyed, refusing to grant him his vision. He tried in vain to bring his heavy breathing under control. No joy there either. His chest rose up and down with the same regularity as a blacksmith's hammer, and to him it seemed just as noisy. He sensed his enemy closing in. Surely now he was doomed. Nothing could, or would, save him. A long hot tongue rasped against his face, tasting, probing.

"Mmm, sweet. I haven't tried blackberry before." The creature said, and with a hearty laugh carried on "Come on Vik you can get up now." A playful nip on his nose saw Vik spring to his feet, his breathing slowly returning to normal.

"Oww! Not so hard Oxy."

"Oh, s-s-sorry!" Oxy stammered. He was on holiday, after all, and Vik's family had kindly given him a nice room with a view. Or should that be nest? For Oxymitrus, as he and his family were known, were rodents from South America, and Vik was his cousin. Vik's tongue washed away the remnants of the blackberry from his furry face. He turned and looked back up the hill. How had he missed it? The blackberry was the size of a pine cone. At least that's what it seemed to him, for everything is much, much bigger if you're a vole.

Cousin Oxy had come for a few week's holiday to escape the terrible rainy season that befalls the South American continent where they normally live. A kind bilge rat had given them passage on a freighter bound for Britain and they had duly arrived, safe and sound, at the small wood, or copse, where Vik and his family lived. Vik had immediately taken a shine to his cousin, bigger than he with bright shiny eyes and a nose that never stopped twitching. He had proudly shown him his domain, his patch. The wood was almost entirely surrounded by wheat and barley fields, far away from the hustle and bustle of cities and towns. A quiet place where only the far-off grumbling of the farmer's tractor could be heard as he cut his crops in readiness for Autumn.

Autumn was a great time for the creatures of the woodland. Mother Nature dropped her bountiful harvest on the copse's carpet of leaves and twigs and so on, every crackling hit alerting the nearby creatures of a possible banquet. Acorns, berries of all kinds, rotten fallen fruit, even the occasional juicy worm or grub, though it was frowned on to take too many worms as they were usually the chosen food of the badgers who also lived here. If they caught you, a painful bite could be expected as punishment. For today though, Vik and Oxy had played a great game of round and round the beech tree, followed by the exhausting game of tag they had just completed. Funny, thought Vik, how it was always his turn to be it.

"Phew, I'm thirsty!" said Oxy.

"Come on then," Vik replied. "I will take you down to the brook, so we can have a drink." Vik's mind was already plotting revenge on his cousin. As Oxy lapped at the water's edge, which Vik knew to be shallow, he would push him in and give him a good soaking. He grinned at the prospect.

What was that noise? Both the little creatures stiffened, not moving, only their noses twitching and their ears rotating, like small radars on the top of an aircraft carrier, as they struggled to pick out that unfamiliar sound. There it was again. Much closer now. Persistent. Getting louder. Still, the little rodents did not move, for if it was trouble, fleeing might draw the attention of whatever was making the noise to them as they made their retreat. Vik trembled, ready to race off in an instant. Still, the rustling came nearer. Finally, after what seemed an age, the leaf litter parted to reveal an oversized stag beetle, his huge shiny mandibles glistening in the autumn sunshine, its weak eyes squinting to try and pick out the two shapes in front of it that had stopped its progress. In truth, its sense of smell was much better than its eyes.

"Vik, is that you?" the creature asked.

"Phew!" Vik and Oxy sank in relief. "S-s-sammy, you gave us quite a fright!" Vik gasped.

"Oh, I'm sorry, I thought I was being quiet."

"Huh! Oxy, meet Sammy the Stag Beetle. He's not much to look at, but he is an old friend of mine and my family." Vik explained. Oxy moved a bit closer. He had never seen a stag beetle before, so named because of the huge antler-like horns on his head.

"You are new," The beetle said, sniffing at Oxy intently. "Where are you from? Oh well, doesn't matter, I must be off. Can't stand around talking all day." He shuffled off, nosing back into the carpet of leaves before Oxy could get out a word.

"Well," Oxy exclaimed, "He was quite a character, wasn't he?"

So, as Vik and Oxy restarted their journey down to the brook Vik told his cousin about the day that Vik and Sammy had become friends. It was in the Spring time, when Vik had just been born. Playful and curious by nature, Vik had one day wondered too far from his parents' nest, and like all children who don't listen to their mums and dads, he had gotten into trouble. Sniffing about and exploring, this way and that, Vik had become ensnared when a bramble had wrapped around his small leg, the tendril digging into his flesh, trapping him. Only a few seconds passed, though to a small vole they seemed an eternity, when along had come Sammy. Quickly sizing up what had happened, and having children of his own, he quickly set about freeing Vik by slicing the sharp bond that restrained the small creature.

"Oh gosh thanks!" Vik had said, a little bit scared, as at that stage of his early life the large and powerful beetle was almost as big as he was.

"No problem, no problem at all" said the beetle. "You must be Vernon's boy."

"I am, yes" said Vik, relieved.

"I know your father well. Still live by that fallen Oak tree?" the beetle casually asked.

"Oh yes!" said Vik, starting to feel talkative.

"Well get back there! Before I tell your father about how far you have strayed, and the trouble I found you in!" roared the beetle. Horrified, Vik wheeled around and fled for home. Vik could not know that the beetle was only joking and liked a good tease. A good tease is what Vik got every time they met after that. It was the basis of a long and strong friendship.

They had reached the water's edge. The grass was slippery from the number of creatures that gathered here to quench their thirst, for although winter was approaching, it had not rained much as yet. The two animals paused carefully, scanning the undergrowth for a menacing predator that fancied vole or such on its menu. Mink, Weasel, Stoat. All preyed upon the animals here. Vik shivered. Sometimes, the woodland could be a dangerous place indeed. He had given up on the idea of drenching his cousin as they neared the cool clear liquid. After all, he had licked nearly all the blackberry off his face. With their thirst quenched, they watched one of the last great crested newts haul itself out of its watery domain, disappearing into a small hole further up the bank in readiness for its winter hibernation.

"It is getting dark now." Vik announced. "Time we headed for home. My mum's got you something special for tea." Oxy's eyes lit up. As if they could get any brighter.

"Oh tell me what it is, what is it?" A playful nudge and Vik pushed him out of the way.

"You'll have to catch me first!" he laughed, as they resumed the game of tag once more. Blissfully unaware now of the impending gloom that dusk brings, they played happily, zigzagging their way back to the huge fallen tree where Vik's family had made their home. They did not have to go far when Vik stopped his frolicking. Where was Oxy? The wood was now deathly quiet. Not a bird called out nor a squirrel chattered. Not even a wood louse stirred. Vik did not move, his small ears stirring to make out a sound, any sound, such as the quiet.

At last, he heard it: a terrible piercing shriek. There it was again, louder, nearer. He panicked.

Jack-knifing into action he plunged forward, all thoughts of staying still vanished from his frightened mind. He could vaguely scent out where his nest and safety lay. He furrowed his way through the carpet of fallen leaves, much the same way as a freighter makes a bow-wave through a choppy sea.

Where was everybody? No-one in sight, no-one to call out to. It was almost dark. Surely the gathering gloom must give him some safety. Just as quickly as he started he stopped again, trembling uncontrollably, vibrating with fear. *Whump, whump, whump.* Seeming to come from directly above him, quickly rising in volume until it was almost deafening. Should he take flight again, or remain motionless? The noise was almost painful in its volume now. He turned to his left, just in time to see a tidal wave of small leaves and twigs engulf him. This new cover was quickly torn away from him. *Thud thud.* He tried to move but could not: he was trapped in a terrifying vice like grip.

Chapter Two: Coming Out

A scaly foot held him securely. Extending from this were talons sharper than a scimitar. As he looked up into the darkness he could see the leg rising to join a body that seemed a long way above him. There was an awful smell coming from this creature of the dark, a scent he had never encountered before; the pungent odour of a terrible predator.

For what seemed an eternity the creature did not move; in reality it was only a matter of seconds. Vik let out a fearful squeal. The creature jerked upwards, the few remaining twigs and small particles of leaf stuck to Vik's body cascading down to the woodland floor, spiralling round and round in much the same way as a mortally wounded insect does during summertime when it has been struck by a swift.

Higher and higher Vik was taken, the downdraft from the creature's wings ferociously fanning him, tornado-like, terrifying him yet further. The creature tilted over sharply, checking its upward momentum, to land quite heavily on a large Oak bough.

Vik was by now semi-conscious, the heavy jolt blasting the air from his lungs. His little heart was gradually slowing down, unable to keep its frantic drummer's beat. He opened his eyes slowly. He felt cold and ached all over. Resigned to his fate now, he scarcely noticed that the sun had risen once more. How much time had passed he had no idea. He could see the beast more clearly now. Creamy white feathers giving way to a darker hue as they rose up its body. A huge head jolted forward then tilted down, gazing directly at him. Piercing predator's eyes, a large hook like beak, pale yellow in colour. Coming nearer, it looked to Vik like it was made to rip its victim's flesh to shreds. He gulped painfully – particularly voles. Its face less than an inch from Vik now, the little vole squeezed his eyes shut, ready for the worst, ready for his life to be ripped from him. He could hear the creature speak, but simply could not bring himself to answer, such was his disbelief.

"I will say it again. Who are you?" the creature asked. Whimpering, incoherent, Vik finally managed a breathless reply.

"I-I-I am Vik the vole." He said. The survival mechanism in his mind sprang into work. Instantly his hopes rose, burning hotter than the sun. If he could keep the creature talking he might have a chance at escape. A quick twist perhaps this way and that to free him. Then he looked down. During his ascent in the dark, the little rodent had no idea how high he had risen. He was impossibly far away from the ground and the safe haven. Escape was definitely not an option. Try to buy more time, yes that was it. Keep this monster from carrying out its most dreadful act, its skill honed by thousands of generations.

"Wuh-wuh, what's your name?" Vik asked tremulously, desperately trying to keep his captor occupied.

"My name is Oswald. Oswald the owl!"

"Owl! Oh no!" sobbed Vik, losing all his control. The tales of these winged marauders of the night, told by a succession of vole grandfathers, had sent many a young vole off to its sleep in the night to wee its bed in a fearful nightmare.

"There there, please don't be frightened." The owl said, in its best soothing manner. "I'm not going to eat you, or kill you, or hurt you. I couldn't." The owl said, brokenly. Amazed, Vik looked up as the owl seemed to shake, juddering in a quite peculiar manner.

His confidence gaining somewhat, Vik asked "Are you alright?"

"Yes, oh yes, I am perfectly fine." The owl looked down at Vik once more, his yellow ringed eyes misted with tears.

"Why are you crying?" the rodent asked, feeling perkier by the second. "Are you hurt?"

"No, no." sighed the owl.

"Then what is it?" Vik demanded. Realising that he'd have to share his sad burden with someone, someday, the owl told the captive vole his secret in a dejected manner.

"I just hoped that I could be like everybody else. To fit in, to go unnoticed, just to be one of the gang." Another sob, and the owl went on, "but that will never be. That will never be. If I told them, the other owls would drive me away, an outcast, unwanted, just like my father."

Vik was thoughtful. He countered "But there's nothing the matter with you. You can fly, speak, hunt, and you terrified me." A sad grin crossed the owl's face.

"Yes, I know. I have learned to keep my secret hidden very well."

His curiosity growing greater by the moment, Vik pleaded "Tell me, please tell me! If I can help in any way, I will. We voles sometimes live in great communities, and we always look out for each other."

"Well they didn't stick by you today." The owl retorted.

Not nearly as frightened now, Vik said "What secret can be so bad as to make a hunter such as you so sad?" So the owl told him, let him have it straight. Vik stared at him in disbelief. The owl repeated himself once more, cautioning Vik, "Not so loud, the others might hear you."

"A vegetarian? A vegetarian!" Vik went on and on, like some broken old gramophone record that had got its needle stuck in a dusty groove. In his short life, he had heard many strange things, but never anything quite like this. The owl had fallen silent now, turning his feathered head around to an impossible degree, which only an owl could do.

He turned back and let out a sigh, saying "The coast is clear, you can go now." He lifted his powerful foot, with all the sensitivity of a skilled surgeon. Instead of beating a hasty retreat along the grooved bough of oak and bolting into the small hole in the trunk he had just spied, Vik felt strangely compelled to stay. Call it fate, or even destiny, he simply could not bring himself to leave. The sun was much higher now, dawn having long gone.

Vik said to Oswald, "Aren't you supposed to sleep in the daytime?"

"I am supposed to yes, though this is when I usually eat." "Eat?" Vik repeated and, after a short pause, said "Eat in the daytime?"

"Yes. There are no other owls about to see me eating the fruits and berries, or perhaps a discarded salad from some picnicker." The owl explained, "I kept you there on the branch knowing that the other owls who hunt this wood should see me and note that I had made yet another kill, when in fact every mouse or vole I take I release, when no-one is looking."

"Huh, well, that is good news! The merciful owl, that's a new one."

Vik was standing up now, stretching his cramped muscles, when an idea struck him. "So you like to eat fruit, and it's important that the other owls don't see you?"

"Yes." said Oswald, with a sad patience.

"Then I know of a place where you can go and eat all you like, in comfort and safety." Oswald seemed to revive before Vik's very eyes.

"Show me, oh show me please! Or at least tell me the direction how to find it." Now if you're a vole, explaining something that is a long way away is a fairly hard thing to do. Vik could hardly say to the owl to turn left at the next large clump of toadstools you see and follow the millipede trail to the edge of the wood. No, there was only one thing for it. Vik would have to take the owl there. Vik explained, the owl listened and agreed. He gently gathered Vik up in one of his muscular talons again, though this time Vik was glad to see that the owl's talons had retracted a bit.

Chapter Three: Blackberries

"Hold on tight," Oswald said.

"I am, I am!" squealed Vik, half in terror, half in excitement. The owl fell forward off the bough as if he'd been shot. Then, effortlessly, with all the grace of one who has been born to fly, he started to beat his wings, catching an updraft from the woodland floor to sustain his height.

To Vik, to travel in this way, in the daylight, to see the bushes and woodland plants below him was fantastically exciting. He felt he would collide with every bush and tree the owl passed. Flying with ghostly stealth, a kaleidoscope of images bombarded Vik. For instance, the look of horror on Roger the rook's face as he saw Oswald flying towards him. The way he banked over, almost vertical, to get out of the owl's way. Then the riot of colour below him as he broke free of the woods and he spied the gorgeous golden-yellow hues of waving wheat beneath, still escaping the farmer's plough, for now. He felt as if he were a deaf composer, hearing a violin for the first time. So this was flying. This was what it felt like to be an owl, to be above the ground. To be safe from predators. "Well, this is definitely for me." He had never thought of himself as a climber on the fruit food chain, but now, after this... well.

The journey seemed endless. Vik had no idea where to go; really, he just knew that when he saw it, he would know when to stop. Suburbia. There it was. The fields of gently swaying crops giving way to parkland or recreational ground, then rows and rows of terraced houses, each backing onto a lane. Over the years, the townsfolk had tipped their unwanted garden rubbish here, all plant cuttings, fertiliser sacks, plastic, corrugated sheets and all broken greenhouse frames. Perfect, just perfect.

"There! Down there!" Vik exclaimed. To Oswald, it looked pretty much like any patch of ground they had covered, but he had a budding trust in the little creature he had clasped securely beneath him. He duly fanned out his wings and tilted them at an angle to halt his momentum, then swooped down to land in an instant. He opened his claw to set Vik free, but for a few long seconds, the little vole could not bring himself to move. He was still saturated in the ecstasy of the owl's graceful flight.

This faded quickly though with Oswald's help, when the owl said, "Come on Vik, I'm starving." Vik then remembered that the owl had not eaten all night. He quickly spied his quarry. He turned to the owl.

"You wait here, and watch out for me, for I am going to gather you a sweet, sweet banquet, just you wait and see." He scurried off a few metres until he reached a large bramble bush. And where there are brambles, at this time of year, there are blackberries, deliciously sweet and rich in energy giving sugars.

It was Vik's turn to exploit the gifts that nature had given him, for these slim tendrils with their crowns of fruit perched high above would not support the weight of a heavy owl. Nor would he be able to pluck the berries from the bush; Oswald's heavy talons were far too large and cumbersome for this delicate and refined work.

For a vole though, it was another matter. He raced up the bramble's thorny stems, with all the speed and purpose of a race horse winner with just a furlong to go. Refinement went out of the window as he neared the first clump of fruit, its heady bouquet wafting forward to greet him, for he too was hungry. He devoured five or six of the purple blackberries without break, then remembered his friend. His speed slowed, he carefully gathered eight or nine berries, wrapped his tail around them and arched his tail over to rest on his back, holding his bounty secure. He expertly traversed the narrow vines till he plunged down at the foot of the spreading thorny bush. With a short scuttle he proudly deposited his bounty at Oswald's feet.

"Try these." Vik said triumphantly. Gingerly, the owl stooped over and picked up one of the berries in him mouth. He gently swallowed, his eyes closing in pleasure.

"Hmmm mmm mmm!" Then in a flash, he gobbled up the rest off the floor. "Wow. What a taste!" Oswald said. "I have sneaked a few gooseberries and once ate a rambler's strawberry which fell out of his basket, but these take some beating. I will have some more." said the bird, nodding back in the direction of the jungle of bramble bushes. The fruit raider's foray was repeated half a dozen times, and still Oswald's appetite showed no signs of diminishing. Vik felt his legs slowly turn into jelly as he dumped down his parcel of fruit once more.

"I will have a rest now, I am shattered." He announced.

"Oh ok, sorry" said Oswald, "I hope you don't think that I am greedy. It is just that I need a lot of fruit to keep me going. I could do with a nap as well."

It was midday now, and the autumn mist that had bathed the woodlands and surrounding fields with its ghostly cloak had departed. There was no breeze and it felt reasonably warm. Vik crawled underneath a large, cracked piece of glass from an old greenhouse to find even more heat.

"Just the job" he sighed contentedly and was soon fast asleep. Oswald too had found a place of refuge to keep him from prying eyes, though unlike Vik his was more the fear of being seen, than being eaten.

Vik awoke with a start. You know when you have that feeling, that sixth sense that something's not right, not as it should be? Well, Vik was feeling it right now. Strongly. He listened intently. Not a sound could be heard. He had no idea how much time had passed. Well, you don't if you're a vole, do you? He called out in a timid voice, "Oswald? Oswald?" squeaking more like a shrew than a vole. Slightly embarrassed, he called again, louder, deeper.

"Oswald, is that you?" No reply, just the increasing sense of unease enveloping him. There was nothing for it but to make a move and see if he could find his winged friend. He edged forward about a millimetre, when he saw it out of the corner of his eye, shooting towards him, with the speed and accuracy of a missile.

Thwack! The creature had not seen the glass. Only the terrified little rodent had been in its sights, and the repulsive thing had already made up its mind that this was dinner. The force of the impact transferred through the glass to shake Vick violently. He could not understand how he had been spared. He could not make sense of this transparent safety shield. And what a safety shield it was! On the other side, the creature fixed him with a pair of cold, black eyes that seemed to emanate evil. At last, galvanised now, he sprang forward half a metre or so, then quickly retreated to spring back the other way. This ruse worked. The larger animal could not check its momentum and carried on for a second or two. All that dodging and running with Oxy was beginning to bear fruit.

In a trice, he emerged from underneath the glass and belted down the narrow path, between some discarded brick. Being so small, even a house brick lying on its side was too high for Vik to quickly vault over and make his desperate way to safety. He was corralled between the narrowing pieces of masonry. He dared not look back. Instinctively, he could feel the monster closing in on him, sense his impending doom a second away. He passed the last dull orange brick and veered sharply to the left, digging his four little feet into the earth, cutting them on hundreds of tiny pieces of broken rubble as he did so. He saw it too late. No escape. A piece of corrugated sheet lay on the broken ground, barring his progress. Emerging expectantly from behind it was another of these vile creatures.

Bigger than the last, as if that were possible, it did not seem to have any legs or arms or whiskers. It simple oozed its way out of its place of concealment. It flicked a forked tongue at him, tasting the air. This was an alley of death for many a small creature that had tried to make its fear riven and forlorn escape, and now it was Vik's turn. Vik slowly inched his head around. Sure enough, the creature that first attacked him had now blocked the narrow exit of the broken brick avenue.

"He's mine." the creature announced to his larger confederate. It spoke in a ghastly, drawling, hissing voice.

"No, you ate first last time." was the equally sinister reply. Both creatures stopped at once. Vik scarcely noticed. *Whump, whump, whump*. The two would-be diners tilted their heads to try and pick out the strange vibrations through the air, which were increasing quite markedly. Stiff with fear, Vik forced his head to look upwards. Never had a vole been so glad to see an owl.

With all the finesse of an African hippopotamus trudging from a day's wallowing in a mud pool, Oswald came to ground. *Bump! Bang!* Lurching forwards to stop himself tipping over, Oswald expertly side slipped a strike from the larger of the two snakes. In a quick breath he called, "Watch out Vik, they're adders! One bite and it's curtains." He quickly swivelled to meet his little friend's tormentors, slowly beating his wings forward, then bringing them back three times as fast to catch out the unwary, smaller snake. *Smack!* The powerful wing made a heavy contact with the back of the reptile's head, slamming it into unconsciousness against the corrugated sheeting that had served them so well before. One against one now.

The owl kept moving in a slow circular motion, trying to flank around the creature that stood in the way of him reaching his mesmerised furry comrade.

"That vole is mine! You catch your own." the snake burbled in its malevolent manner. The snake could not guess, could not know, that Oswald wanted to reach the vole to save him, not devour him. Vik watched as the large adder uncoiled and drew itself up to its full height, level with his feathered saviour. He watched helplessly, terrified as combat was joined.

The ghastly reptile lunged at the owl, to be parried away. Oswald was well aware that one poisonous bite from this dark, zig-zag marauder would be a certain if slow death for himself and an even swifter one for Vik. For four or five long minutes they sparred, neither animal gaining the upper hand.

To the tiny rodent watching them, it seemed like hours. Vik had tried to shout encouragement to squeal and distract the snake. No such luck. His throat was refusing to work, remaining as dry as the wind-burnt northern steppe. Finally, a piece of luck fell the adder's way, butting his head forward at the ferociously flapping owl, he made contact with Oswald's stomach, hitting him with all the force of an anti-tank shell. The air exploding from his lungs, he flipped over backwards to lie face down, motionless.

Turning with a triumphant air, the adder moved slowly towards Vik, twisting left and coiling right in an effort to hypnotise the terrified little creature. All that exertion had made the powerful snake even more hungry, the pit of its stomach burning hotter than a furnace. The snake reared up to strike, to finish Vik. Already salivating, he could almost taste the vole. In an instant, the look of hungry intent was wiped from the adder's face: closing around its thick neck like a padlock snapping shut were the courageous owl's talons.

"Down but not out." said Oswald, with steely determination, as he jerked skywards with a powerful motion. A few feet in the air, and the owl twisted quickly, sending its adversary gyrating through the air to impale itself horrible on the needle-sharp skewers of a black thorn bush. One convulsion and the awful snake dropped its head for the last time, the life going out of its eyes.

Oswald sat down exhausted. At last, free from his fear, Vik danced over to greet his tired friend. "You did it, you did it!" Cried the vole, warm relief surging through his veins. Oswald took a few seconds to compose himself, then gasped to Vik, for he was still breathing very hard.

"Let's get out of here. This place gives me the creeps." Vik dived into one of the open claws and in no time, Oswald quickly rocketed them into the sky and safety. Both Vik and Oswald agreed that they had paid a heavy price for collecting such a sugar rich bounty as the ripe blackberries.

"Something a lot easier next time," said Oswald.

"And safer!" chipped in Vik. They both chuckled at that.

It was getting dark now. Mother Nature drew her dark veil across the countryside. Oswald's keen eyesight, precise as a laser, had picked out what he thought would give them a secure and safe night's sleep. A partly fallen stone wall, jutting up into the sky, was full of warm nooks and crannies where the two comrades could gather a much-needed rest. This turned out to be a good move, made even greater by the fact that some kind creature had stored a meal of nuts and strange looking berries in one of the gaps at the top of the wall, still radiating heat from the afternoon's sunlight. The two hungry animals made short work of the delicious harvest, delightedly stuffing themselves until they could feast no more.

"How did you know that this place would make such a good shelter?" asked Vik sleepily.

"I am a Barn Owl," said Oswald. "This is the kind of home I would always choose, quiet and secluded."

"Hmm." said Vik. The Vole went on "what did you think of those green berries?"

"Lovely and sweet." answered Oswald.

"What were they? Dried grapes?" said Vik, trying to sound knowledgeable. "I think they are called raisins, or sultanas, or something like that."

"Whatever." sighed Oswald, contentedly. "I would not mind more of them tomorrow."

"Well," said Vik, coming alive at the thought of yet more food, "It so happens I know of a place where they grow fresh, the fruit hanging from the vines like giant pine cones! Or so I am told by my grandfather. Easy to find, as well." Oswald was about to enthusiastically throw himself in with the idea, then remembered this afternoon's adventure.

"After today's idea, I think I will pass. I have had enough excitement for a bit." He laughed to himself, then dropped his head and fell into a deep sleep, still standing the way only an owl could do.

Chapter Four: Grapes and Greenhouses

The following morning was a different day altogether. Heavy, driving rain raked the land, like countless machine guns stinging and slashing at the earth. They had both slept very well, Vik stretching lazily, opening his eyes to find Oswald looking out of their gap in the stone fortress, trying to gather raindrops in his ungainly beak.

Seeing this, Vik gathered a leaf off the floor of the shelter. He rolled it with great skill to make a kind of cigar shaped tube. He then scooped up an empty acorn cup, which they had eaten the previous evening, and scurried over to Oswald, motioning him to get out of the way. He moved forward, sticking his two front legs out into the freezing rain, the tube catching the small drops of water the same way a small net catches a tadpole. He held the high end of the tube facing into the wind and rain, and the bottom end over the acorn cup, which he had placed upturned on the floor. Very soon the cup had filled, to be drank then filled again. In a short time, both Oswald and Vik's thirsts were quenched.

Sometime later, the skies were growing lighter. Oswald squinted out and announced, "It will stop raining in a short while." Vik did not mind. He was more than warm, snuggled under one of Oswald's generous wings. The two animals chatted back and forth. Vik sleepily let Oswald ramble on, then bolted upright, trying to clear himself from the massive feathered wing cloaking him.

"What was that you said Oswald? Repeat that!" Vik demanded, urgently.

"I said," repeated Oswald, "That one of my cousins had caught a strange kind of mouse from the woodland floor, not too far away from where I found you. He was an odd-looking thing. Said he was on holiday from South America, would you believe? You rodents will try anything to escape being eaten." Horrified, Vik realised it was Oxy. So that was why Oxy had not answered him when he'd called out. He had been taken.

Vik could hardly bring himself to ask the question, for it hardly seemed likely that there were two vegetarian owls in one wood. "Has he been eaten? Is he alive?" he questioned.

"Certainly he is alive," replied Oswald, "any new creature that is found by the brotherhood of owls is taken to the dark chasm, kept there until Tremidious the Terrible arrives to see him and decide his fate."

"Tremidious the Terrible?" repeated Vik weakly, his early relief that his cousin was alright fading slightly.

"Yes, Tremidious is a giant Tawny owl, sometimes he catches and kills two mice at once! He is a fearful predator of your kind." Oswald went on.

"How long has he got?" Vik questioned.

"Two, maybe three days. Very few creatures are spared. Tremidious usually comes with one of his many brides, and the captive is given up as a sweet feast in the hope that the bride will bear him many sons."

Vik breathed in deeply. Such was the way his life had turned around, and at such pace, he had hardly given his cousin, or indeed his family, a second thought, for voles are not usually recognised as the most intelligent of creatures. Vik, however, was very bright for a Vole.

After a short pause, he said "I have got a plan Oswald. You'll have to help me." This last was more a statement of fact than a request for help. So, a plan was hatched. First, they would go in search of the sweet grapes that had given them such sustenance the night before, then try and rescue Oxy, before the chief of owls arrived with his new brides and his bodyguards.

Oswald knew that the time had come to stand up and be counted. Or rather, fly. If the other owls turned their backs on him and made him an outcast for helping this little vole and his cousin, then so be it. Better to be yourself and have one or two friends than live life in a lie and be desperately lonely and unhappy.

The sun was now breaking free from the cold autumn shower clouds, so they made ready. Gathered once more in Oswald's firm grip, Vik again experienced the terrifying yet exciting sensation of flight that Oswald employed effortlessly, plunging vertically down from the wall, then pulling up to level out only millimetres from the ground. Vik felt he had to close his mouth to prevent his wildly beating heart from jumping out of his body. Gradually, his heartrate returned to normal. He was now able to appreciate and marvel at the sights around him.

Oswald, his wings beating tirelessly in majestic rhythm, seemed oblivious to it all. He gently altered the angle of his wings to take them higher, to meet the treetops. Now, rising up beneath them was a lush green field, with peculiar black and white beasts gently ambling along, stopping now and then to crop the grass.

"Cows," Oswald said, in anticipation of Vik's next question. Now he had relaxed, Vik had launched a barrage of enquires at the owl. Oswald had given up trying to explain what they were, what they did or where they had come from. He just answered with one word for the inquisitive little vole, with all the patience of a grandfather taking his grandson to the zoo for the first time.

The owl would repeat the word so that Vik could take the information onboard.

"Butterfly."

"Starlings."

Below them, a panic-stricken creature startled by the sound passing overhead broke out of its cover, squawking raucously.

"Pheasant."

"Drab coloured Hen, trying to find flight."

Then, another exclamation from Oswald, "Swifts!"

To Vik, these small birds were truly something to wonder at, as they wheeled around, dived and climbed spitfire like, as they feasted on their prey of winged insects.

"They can fly better than you!" Vik cried.

"That's true," said Oswald, "they are the buccaneers of the sky. Soon, they will leave this country for a warmer sun, all the way to Africa."

Much higher now and the thick tree cover they were passing over was gradually giving way to more broken ground; hedges, bushes and whatnot, until the flat, geometric pattern of an ornamental garden, a riot of colour, unfurled beneath them. Banking over gently, Oswald changed direction once more. The elegant and imposing lines of a country house came into view. Losing height now, Oswald glided over an ornamental pond, full of fat goldfish. They looked like so many bright carrots in the green soupy water.

Taking care not to collide with any of the dragonflies that hovered just above the pond's surface, Oswald tilted over sharply to round the house and home in on their intended target. He landed on a large chestnut tree as gently as a dew drop hitting a spider's web. Well camouflaged in the jungle of leaves, the two creatures spied the lie of the land.

A long, L-shaped greenhouse harboured the coveted, ripe, juicy berries. Not only grapes were grown in the greenhouses artificial climate but tomatoes the size of golf balls and some peculiar looking plants also. After a careful inspection, Oswald could see a way in. Some of the greenhouse's uppermost windows were ajar, in an effort to gain some fresh air and prevent the greenhouse from becoming too hot. Here, Vik and Oswald agreed that they would make their entrance to the vast, juicy treasure house.

They waited while an old balding gardener ambled past, his shoulders stooped by many years of work among the flower beds. His faded waistcoat and grubby white shirt were testament to the fact that he would do many a day's battle with the unrelenting weeds and pests that sought to invade and colonise this tranquil paradise.

As he rounded the corner out of sight, the pair sprang into action. Or perhaps 'flapped' would be a better word. Alighting gingerly on the slippery glass, Oswald released Vik from his grip. The angle was not too steep, so Vik half-slithered, half-scampered down the open window pane and looked inside.

Here before him was indeed a breath-taking sight. As far as his little eyes could see were scores of large grapes bunched together among the bright green vine leaves, just begging to be plucked, begging to be eaten. Even the hanging gardens of Babylon could not have looked as good as this.

Then further off were the tomatoes, growing from the tomato plants arrested mid-air like some fast bowler's cricket-ball. Red as rubies, Vik found the heady scent of this fruit intoxicating, overpowering. He had to grip the edge of the glass to stop himself swooning to the floor of soft peat, earth and compost below.

"Well what do you see?" asked Oswald, impatiently waiting behind him, his hungry stomach starting to beat louder and louder like some brass band's bass drum.

"Fooood!" gasped Vik. "We're going in!" Very carefully the owl relinquished his grip and with his head nudged the glass open still further. He could feel the heat emanating from below.

He could smell the delicious bouquet of berries beneath him. If his stomach was beating loudly before, it was now rivalling Big Ben. The owl said "Hold on to my back tight Vik. I will need both feet for this." Vik quickly ascended the owl's proffered wings then climbed onto his back, grasping the feathers as tight as he could.

Head down, Oswald and Vik plunged inside. Vik guided Oswald to the ripest and sweetest of the grapes. After slashing at the bunches with Oswald's powerful talons, the pair watched the grapes fall to Earth, thudding against the soft soil beneath, like small conkers falling from their tree.

The owl set a frantic pace, for neither of the two animals felt comfortable in this confined space. "I think that's enough," Vik said to Oswald, "that's about as much as we can carry."

"Good" said Oswald, "we will eat some here and take the rest with us for later." The two creatures set to work gobbling up the sweet fruit with all the appetite of a pair of locusts. Juice running down their mouths, stomachs bulging, Oswald said to Vik between munches, "Now this is an adventure."

Full to the brim, Oswald began to wonder if he would be able to fly with all the food he had eaten, the food he wanted to carry and then there was Vik. Vik did not look like a vole, so much as a furry fattened peach, with ears and whiskers one end and a tail at the other.

A sharp *tap-tap-tap* made them freeze, become immobile. This was not the type of tapping of a creature on the prowl, more a desperate beating of one who is panicking, terrified. Trapped.

Without so much as saying a word, Oswald launched upwards, grabbing Vik as he did so. In a trice he had manoeuvred the pair through the enlarged opening at the top of the green house.

"See what it is" ordered Vik. Oswald turned on a fifty pence piece to wheel around and head along the roof of the clean glass building. They could still hear the tapping even through the thick glass. Turning to follow the contour of the L-shaped building they alighted gently down, right above the section which held the bulging ripe tomatoes. His keen hearing guiding them unerringly, Oswald had put them right above the noise.

Beneath them was a sight indeed. Its legs and one wing tangled in an unruly role of chicken wire was a huge crow, its powerful black beak was hammering against the glass in its frenzy to be free.

Noticing the movement above, the crow called out with a piteous cry "Help me, save me, please!" The feeling of being trapped was one that the vole knew well. Only the day before it had been his turn to be caught, to be plucked from the safety of the woodland's leaf litter to what Vik thought would be a petrifying finale to his young life.

Sympathising with the creature struggling below him, he said to Oswald, "Well don't just stand there, let's set him free."

"What about the rest of the grapes?" Oswald asked.

Vik's reply was terse, "No chance of getting any more of them 'till we stop the row he is making. He will alert everybody near."

Another effortless take off and Oswald plunged back down into the greenhouse with all the purpose of a stealth bomber on its final run before realising its bombs. He pulled up so sharply that Vik, his grip tested to the limit, nearly shot forward over and into the relieved and enmeshed bird, much the same way an excited child falls off a seaside donkey at his first attempt. Gasping in between laboured breath, the crow managed to blurt out a grateful thanks. Slowly he managed to vanquish his panic.

Vik had let go his tenuous grip on the owl. Springing into action he carefully unravelled the thin, but strong, wire that had enveloped the bird.

"What's your name? Crow, do you have a name?"

Nearly free now and quickly regaining his composure the crow drew himself to his full height and announced in a well-spoken accent "Caruthers, Caruthers the crow."

"Glad to meet you" said Vik, still toiling and twisting the wire away from the one remaining foot that was trapped. "My name's Vik and his name's Oswald."

"Very glad to make your acquaintance. I was really frightened!" the shiny black bird told them. He went on to tell them that like all members of the crow family, magpies, the more secretive Jay and so on, he was naturally curious. So, when he happened along and noticed the greenhouse, felt the warm air with all its fruity fragrance wafting up to meet him, drawing him down and into the confined space, where he felt sure that a sweet surprise awaited him.

Well he got a surprise all right, but certainly not sweet. His eyes and stomach bulging in unison, he headed straight for the heavy tomatoes, hanging enticingly before him. Trouble was, having never encountered one before, he had no idea of its weight.

As he twisted the juicy red fruit from its perch, the tomato has dragged him straight downwards, like a cannonball, thrown over the side of a ship and into the water. Having no intention of relinquishing his prize, he had plummeted down. Instead of making contact with the soft peat and fertiliser that adorned most of the floor of the greenhouse, he had crashed into the wire.

He had certainly let go of his booty by now, but in his struggle to roll off his back and take flight he had become caught in the beastly stuff. The more he struggled the more he became entangled. "That's where you came in." he gratefully ended.

Free at last, he looked up at the imposing owl and its tiny furry confederate. The crow went on "What, are you saving him for later? Supper or something?" he added curiously.

"No indeed, he's not" answered Vic. "We are partners."

"Par-par-par-" The crow could not bring himself to finish. Finally, managing to complete the word partners, he laughed raucously in disbelief, rocking forwards and backwards in mirth.

Oswald scowled at Vik and bent lower to hoot, "It's supposed to be a secret remember."

"Oh, sorry Oswald" replied Vik, "I told you that voles can sometimes be forgetful."

"Not when it comes to food" Oswald bit back.

Seeing that they were serious, the crow stifled its laughter, observing "Well I have never heard anything to beat that. An owl and a vole! Partners, friends, allies."

"Well it's true," the owl said sternly. "Tell anyone and I will give you a bash with my beak." The crow looked at the powerful owl and agreed to silence immediately. The conversation began flowing freely after Vik's gaffe.

The crow asked, "were you after the tomatoes then?"

"No" said Oswald, "we were after the grapes."

"The grapes!" both the owl and vole exclaimed together. Becoming engrossed in conversation with the crow after his rescue, Vik and Oswald had forgotten their objective. Time was ticking and their mission to save Oxy far from completed. Vik rapidly told the crow about why they were here and what their aim was. Feeling honour bound to help this gallant pair, the crow solemnly swore that he would help to free Oxy from his terrible plight, if that was alright with them.

"Done!" they both said as one.

"Right" said Vik, "back to the grapes."

The crow and owl stood patiently on the greenhouse floor while Vik loaded them with as many grapes as he could. Stuffing them between tight feathers and anywhere else he could find.

"Not there!" said Oswald "I for one will certainly not eat that grape."

"Oh! S-s-s-sorry" said Vik, getting carried away. He tossed the grape over his shoulder. It bounced slightly as it hit the soft earth below, its momentum stopping quickly as it hit something – something furry.

"That will do old chap," Caruthers commented down to Vik, "any more and I will fly like a stone. Had enough of that for one day my man." the crow announced, his non-stop flow of well-spoken conversation continuing.

"Ready Vik?" said Oswald.

"Ready" was Vik's reply as he felt the owl's talons close around him, the other talon holding yet another bunch of the bulbous, sweet fruit they had purloined. Indeed, it seemed as if they had taken half of the greenhouse's generous crop. Heavily laden, the two birds took flight.

So heavy were they that flying straight up and out of the open window pane was an impossibility. They would have to lumber off back down the greenhouse towards the tomatoes. Then, with altitude and speed gained would turn, or try to turn, sharply and head back up the greenhouse for the final time. A swift change of trajectory and they would burst out into freedom to fly back to a safe roost and finish off the rest of their spoils. Vik could feel the resistance of the warm, moist air on his face as they picked up speed. Phase one, nearly completed. Good.

Like a film slowly being sped up, he watched as the tomatoes loomed nearer and nearer. Just when it seemed they would crash kamikaze like into them, the owl stood on its powerful wing, banked over and flew backwards towards the open glass. Vik opened his eyes with heavy relief. He opened them even wider as he saw what was about to unfold.

Following the lighter and more agile crow, Oswald and Vik were no more than four feet above the greenhouse floor. Running parallel with the owl's beating wings were the gardener's trestle tables, on which were kept some of the tools and plant cuttings. Rampaging through them with the speed and purpose of a Serengeti cheetah was a huge Tawny cat, its eyes fixed firmly on Oswald. And it was gaining.

Desperately trying to scream, Vik could not make himself heard against the noise of the owl's furiously beating wings. Oswald's eyes firmly fixed on the glass escape hatch above them. He was composing himself for the split second when he must change the angle of his flight and burst out to freedom.

Vik watched helplessly as the tornado like Tawny closed the gap to them. His face was scarred by many a midnight skirmish with other tomcats, trying and failing to make a foray through his territory, for this was his territory. He had waited quietly outside the greenhouse as Vik and Oswald had made their dramatic entrance. Shaded by a sprawling caster oil bush, he had spied them distracted, freeing the crow which should have been rightfully his, a hearty supper which he would share with one or more of his harem of mistresses.

He crawled the length of the greenhouse, slipping in with deathly stealth, using the cover of the vines to slink closer and closer. Just as he began to crouch, to bunch the muscles in his legs for a formula one like surge, he was struck by the foul-smelling grape that Vik had tossed over his shoulder, which had hit him squarely in the eye. The cat had retracted sharply back into cover. Inching forward once more, he frustratedly looked up as the fruit bearing convoy had winged over and away from him. Then, as if fate had given him a furry stroke of luck, he watched as they turned back towards him.

Years of experience told him to wait until the crow had flown past. Then, as the more weighty, cumbersome and heavily laden owl was passing, he leapt onto the tables and broke into stride with all the verve of an Olympic hurdler. Head down, determined, boring into the slight lead Oswald had.

Vik, realising that Oswald could not hear his terrified screams, knew there was only one thing for it. He sank his teeth into the owl's scaly foot.

"Arrgh!" wailed the owl, his concentration broken, angrily looking down at Vik. His anger dissipated in a moment by the look on the little vole's face, jabbing his front leg back in the direction of the furry foe nearly upon them. Oswald's eyes widened as he saw the determined tawny about to time his leap. No time to think, Oswald used his quick reflexes to try and avert disaster, flicking his large foot out backwards, he fired his cargo of grapes into the face of the cat, where they exploded, Exocet like.

"Meeeaaow!" the cat shrieked, as he careered off the table, crashing into half a dozen clay pots and shattering them with the force of him impact. Squinting upwards, Vick closed his eyes once more, the owl arching upwards towards the open pane. Surely the angle was too tight, they would never make it!

Thwak! Oswald's foot jarred against the pane. Such was the force, Vik was nearly shaken free. He clung on, determinedly, his rapid breathing puffing his chest in and out like a set of bagpipes. The cooler autumn air told the shaken little vole that they had made it. A few brief seconds of laboured flight and they returned to the very same bough of the chestnut tree that they had alighted on before. A few moments passed, and they were joined by Carruthers.

"I thought owls were supposed to be graceful creatures, the swans of the night!" the crow squawked.

"You try flying like a swan with a fat, ferocious moggy on your tail!" said Vik.

"A cat in the greenhouse?" said the crow.

"Yes," the vole went on, "it was nearly curtains."

"Well don't be frightened," said Oswald, justifiably proud of himself. "I had it all under control."

Vik blurted, "Control! control! You didn't even see that cat until it was nearly too late. Let me tell you it's a lot more frightening if you're nearer the ground to see it." The two birds laughed at the vole's recounting of the chase. Their mirth increased when, whilst still resting, they saw one of the gardeners carry the cat out of the greenhouse by the scruff of its neck and give it a swift kick, propelling it into a large bed of mint.

"Thar! That's for damaging those pots and making a mess of his lordship's vines! They be in a right state. Wait till I tell Adge what you been up to!"

They had rested in the tree overnight, the owl and the crow oblivious to the cool night air, though for a small vole like Vik, it was a different matter. No warm burrow, no bed of straw or leaves.

"I am cold." He repeated at short intervals, making sure that both his feathery comrades heard him. At last, seeing his own good night's sleep vanishing, Oswald gently proffered a warm, feathered wing to Vik to snuggle under. Vik dived under the wing quicker than a bullet from a gun, though it was in his nature to fidget and move around, keeping Oswald awake.

This was made much worse when a dog fox came courting, looking for a receptive vixen he could woo, his amorous cries piercing the autumn night like a fairground klaxon. Finally, he stopped to scratch his back against the impressive girth of the giant beech, before meandering off into the woods, his cries still very loud as he drew away.

Chapter Five: Spook

Dawn broke to find Oswald tired. He opened a blurry eye to see the gardens and greenhouses shrouded in a cool mist, through which he could make out a hedgehog late from his night's wondering, heading for his snug home under a nearby laurel hedge.

"I bet he will sleep better than me." Oswald grumbled to himself. He lifted his wing, his warm eider down of feathers, off the vole. Vik, sensing the change of temperature straight away, slowly wakened. "Sorry to disturb you your lordship, but its morning."

"Oh, Oh," mumbled Vik, still drowsy, finally opening his eyes fully. He grinned up at the owl who stared back frostily. In no uncertain terms he told Vik that he would not allow Vik to disturb him like that again. Next night, he was on his own. To Vik, the owl's complaining was like a parent berating a child. The vole could hear, but took no notice, making matters worse by yawing while Oswald was in full flow.

Seeing he was having no effect, Oswald rounded on Caruthers who was still sound asleep, the crow waking as soon as the owl nudged him. Jumping to his feet, Caruthers quickly said, "No time for breakfast Oswald old man, time to be off."

Oswald was about to tell him that he was not going to offer the liquorish coloured bird breakfast, when he reverted to type, gave up good naturedly, and said "Ok, yes let's go."

They had been airborne for about half an hour now, flying through the cool early morning air. Oswald, feeling a little bit guilty for the way he had spoken to his tiny companion, spoke in a muted voice so that Caruthers couldn't hear.

"Look Vik, about this morning. I am sorry I was so grumpy, but I have got used to having a good night's sleep, so I, and well, quite frankly, the way you kept moving around meant I did not get a very good rest." No reply from Vik. Stony silence from the vole, clasped firmly in the owl's foot.

"I said I'm sorry!" Oswald exclaimed again, this time louder, more firmly. Still no response from the sulking vole. "Alright then," surrendered the owl. "I tell you what, to cheer you up, we will play a game."

"A game!" repeated Vik, the vole's curiosity instantly aroused.

"A game?" said Caruthers; funny how the crow seemed to have selective hearing.

"Yes, a game." Oswald went on. "It's usually good fun. It's called 'Spook'."

"Spook?" the vole and crow spoke at once. Now at last, the vole had forgotten his sulks, and the crow's hearing had been magically restored. Oswald outlined the game. Now Spook could be great fun, or rather terrifying, or exciting, depending on how you looked at it.

It quite simply was this: the owl would dive down from his high path in the clouds, screaming and shrieking as he did so, tilting over vertically, gaining great speed. Then, as he approached his target, his unwilling playmate, he would slow down somewhat, giving the panic-stricken creature below, usually rabbit, or even better, a hare, a chance to escape, to race across the field, usually better because they could not find cover so easily, so the game went on even longer. The more shrieks of terror that mortified little creatures gave out, the more points you got, and every now and then, one of these unfortunate little animals would trip and go sprawling face-first into a cowpat. Now that, that was an outright win.

The rules explained to them, both Vik and Caruthers quivered with excitement, though Oswald explained that this was a game better suited to a few owls rather than just one. Five or ten minutes passed, then the owl saw what he was looking for: a large, green grassed earthen bank, rising from a corner of one of the fields they were passing overhead.

Changing direction, he glided around and round with the crow following. It was easier to stay airborne in the warming air now, the sun gaining in strength all the time. The sky, for the moment, was cloudless. The heat from the ground, not very strong, but still radiating upwards nevertheless. The bank offered a good all-round view. The closely cropped grass held patches of Sphagnum moss, the soil made acidic from the constant urination on these patches by the inhabitants; a sure sign that rabbits had heavily colonised the earthen mound.

Everywhere he looked, Vik could see the runs, heading to and away from this lagomorph metropolis. His eyes as precise as a digital camera, Oswald at last spotted a group of four rabbits busily harvesting the unrelenting bounty of grass beneath them. Having done this many times before, he ignored Vik's excited plea.

"Well, are we going to play, or not?"

Oswald did not answer. He knew that they were near to cover and would vanish as skilfully as a jewel thief evading a policeman's torch. No, patience is the name of the game. A few more moments and the owl spotted his quarry.

"There!" he said, in a commanding voice. Vik and Caruthers could see a large, confident buck rabbit. This mature male was well established in the rabbits' social hierarchy. To prove his courage, his bravery, he had wondered well out into the field, busily attacking the short stubby crop of cabbages, due to be harvested any day now. He knew that over a short distance he could out-accelerate any fox or poacher's lurcher that might try and tackle him. He had a burst of speed that was truly electric. These fields were well away from any disturbances, so the rabbits were encouraged to stay out much later than they normally would, often after eating, gambolling in play until nearly midday.

Besides, the crop was so short that any marauder would stick out for miles. An airborne assault? That was another matter.

Above the rabbit, Oswald was ready. He had expertly gauged that if he approached from the great grass bank, he would drive the rabbit out into the field of crops still further, so prolonging the game. Nearly ready now, Caruthers closing on his tail like a dutiful wingman. A sharp intake of breath, then the owl hooted, "Tally-ho!"

Nosing down, the two birds, with Vik clutched tightly in Oswald's claws, rocketed towards the hapless, unsuspecting rabbit. Levelling out just above the rabbits' haven of the bank, they tore through the air, low to the ground now. A quick glance from Oswald, and all three let out a banshee cry that would disturb the dead.

"Whheeeee!"

The rabbit, stranded out in the field, could see his fellows exploding into terrified action as they darted this way and that, disappearing into cover in a matter of seconds. The unpleasant realisation that this awful wailing was coming towards him and coming towards him very fast, made the rabbit sit bolt upright, large, furry ears twisting agitatedly to try and pinpoint the sound.

Then, he saw them: a feathered, winged devil with a smaller beast in tow, screaming, flying straight at him like some old World War Two Stuka. Now was the time he would put his finely-honed sprinting speed into practice. The rabbit shot forward, turbo charged in his acceleration. He could not know that this was exactly what his pursuers wanted.

Though he could have swiftly caught him, Oswald slowed now to prolong the chase. The rabbit was emitting a terrified squeal, alerting his brethren in the surrounding fields. He plunged on, crashing through the rows of cabbages, Oswald closing, but deliberately not getting too near.

To Vik, clenched tightly in the Owl's undercarriage, this was tremendously exhilarating. The rows of dark green cabbages flashed quickly underneath him. Like the cat's-eyes placed in the middle of the road, illuminated in the speeding car's headlights, the way the rabbit opened and closed his legs at such high speeds was almost hypnotic, his brown-white tail bouncing rhythmically.

Like all good things that come to an end and leave you wanting more, or perhaps a repeat, the rabbit finally made the cover of a large black thorn bush, diving into sanctuary faster than an arrow. The flight slowed now, as they lifted over the large expanse of blackthorn, angling over slightly to round a stumpy tree, excited and happy. Oswald had been right. Spook had been great fun! The now not so brave rabbit: definitely spooked.

They cleared the field of cabbages, spirits high. The next field to fly over was huge.

"I have never seen one as big!" declared Caruthers. He went on, "Tell you what, let's take a break. It is deeply ploughed, I might be able to find a couple of juicy fat worms for us."

"Oh no thanks." Vik and Oswald said at once, "Not very hungry."

"Well I am. You are always hungry when you are a crow." Coming in to land, they surveyed the field's huge, orderly furrows, cut by the tractor's plough which ran side by side, easily towering above the two birds. It looked a menacing place for someone like Vik. It was a dark, moist, slippery alley, the odd sharp stone stuck out here, a tangle of greasy interlaced roots there. Definitely not a place he would enjoy travelling through. He momentarily shivered; thank goodness they could fly.

There was the occasional dandelion patch further out in the centre of this giant field, strangely uneaten, not bothered by the hordes of rabbits.

"That is peculiar." Caruthers noted.

"You don't sound as if you're from this part of the country. Have you been here long?" Oswald asked the crow.

"No, not that long. Used to live in London. Fantastic living there, but unfortunately my family lost a boundary dispute with a pair of falcons, so we split up and I came here, with my two nephews, Cadwalader and Carstairs. Decent chaps, you will like them when we meet. They are out meeting the crows that live here, get to know them, you understand?"

On the far side of the field, a large burgundy red dog fox emerged. Oswald saw him first with his keen owl's eyesight. He came towards them nearly, but not quite, hidden in the dark furrows. He was big and looked powerful. Clearly, he was in his prime. He made no attempt at concealment, just cut the distance to them with a slow, deliberate gait.

The trio watched him come closer and closer. Without saying a word Oswald and Caruthers prepared for flight. The fox stopped, looked directly at them, and spoke with a leader's authority.

"I hope you enjoyed scaring our food like that." He paused, then went on, "Not something we welcome around these parts. You might have damaged one of our rabbits, one we might feast on in the future. There will be a price to pay." He said, with finality.

Chapter Six: Running the Furrow

"Now look old man, we did not mean any harm you know. Just a bit of youthful fun, ok?" said Caruthers.

"No. I am afraid not." the fox replied. "Often one of you owls would take a small levirate and kill it. Our flock, our stock, as they say."

"What is to stop us taking off and leaving? You are just a little too far away to catch us." Vik ventured.

"I see," said the fox. "A plucky vole. You are a long way from safety anyway. Why haven't you been eaten?"

"Keeping him for later." Oswald said, blithely.

"You are very brave, considering you will be dinner very soon. But in answer to your question, look at all the hedges around this field." A sharp, involuntary intake of breath from Caruthers as he looked out at the field's boundaries. They were surrounded by more than a dozen buzzards, which were perched on the hedges about them, all staring intently at them. Expectantly.

"You see old chap," the fox replied with sarcasm, to match Caruthers' accent, "Here we are a collaboration, a contingent if you will. We all pull together for the benefit of each other. You have had your sport, your fun. Now, we will have ours. If you try to flee, you will all be torn to ribbons. So, make your choice. Face certain death or play in a game of chance."

"What game?" Oswald asked.

"We call it, 'Run the Furrow'." Replied the fox, a slow grin running across his jaws, showing a row of sharp, canine teeth.

"It would be suicide!" said Oswald. "Neither the crow nor I can move very fast."

"We were not thinking of you." He paused, "But your little friend? Just perfect." The three friends, gradually becoming aware that not only did they have a dozen hungry raptors and a large fox to contend with, but behind them, emerging wraithlike from the surrounding furrows, were all manner of predators: ferrets, stoats and a particularly terrifying weasel, who wore his battle-scarred face with some pride. He had never lost this game and was a consummate competitor. He was hopeful he would be picked. As if reading his thoughts, the fox said, "No, not you. You are too big. It will be over too quickly. We want the sport to last, after all."

The fox looked back to Vik. "Well rodent, what is it going to be? Choose. Decide."

"Don't!" whispered Oswald. "We have an outside chance to get away."

"No, we don't." conceded Vik. "Those buzzards will tear us to pieces. One of those birds is much bigger than you. To take them on would be certain death for all of us, and for my cousin."

"He's right my friend," said Caruthers. "It's the only chance we have."

Before Oswald could dissuade him, Vik answered "I will do it." A great roar of approval from the encircling animals told the three of their unbridled, expectant delight. The fox's grin grew even wider, as if that were possible.

"Good, good." He drooled, with obvious satisfaction. "Now let me see who will be your opponent."

There was near hysteria from the remaining malicious Mustelids, though the weasel remained downcast and sullen.

"You. You will do it." The fox jabbed one of his front paws at a particularly lithe, chocolate brown ferret. The chosen adversary could hardly conceal his delight. "Now then," the fox continued, "there is one rule, and one rule only." He looked directly at Vik. "You start at this end of the furrow, and you must make it to the other end. If you try and escape by attempting to go over the top..." he waited a few moments, "Well, need I say more? You will be given a head start. Then the game will begin."

The atmosphere around the large field was electric. "Take your positions." There was a flurry as the buzzards and remaining stoats and ferrets lined themselves across the top of the chosen furrow, either side, each ready to cheer, squeal and shriek with delight, hoping that the kill would be made directly underneath them.

"Right," said the fox, with obvious pleasure, "Shake paws, and we will start." Vik was shivering, but he knew that he had to keep his composure, or it would be game over for his comrades and himself. He started to take in sly little intakes of breath to preload his lungs for the dynamic action he was about to undertake. The ferret came towards him. He looked huge, so much longer than Vik.

"See you in the furrow, vole." He grinned, deliberately showing his teeth to intimidate Vik even further.

Vik thought about his family back in his home wood. His cousin and the two friends waiting for him, friends who had only tried to help him. It calmed him slightly.

"On the count of fifty, you go after him." the fox ordered.

"I understand," said the chocolate brown beast, "I am ready."

Vik took one last look down the furrow. The buzzards spread out either side and the pairs of gleaming eyes just peering over the top, all waiting for his demise. He drew as much breath as he could, then turned, nodded at the fox, and said, "I am ready also."

"Ok. Set, and go!" roared the fox.

Vik exploded forward, his small size giving him instant acceleration. The noise inside the furrow was deafening, he could hear nothing but the screams from his enemy. There was no chance of him hearing the fox counting down, but perhaps that was a good thing. He plunged forward for what seemed an age, his small rodent's muscles burning, his sinews seeming to scream in pain, but he must keep on, there must be no relenting.

The roar, the din, increased even more, the buzzards flapping their wings above him with ferocious glee. This told him that his enemy was in pursuit. Vik knew he could not keep this pace up for much longer. Voles are not built for out and out sprinting. If he carried on this way, it would be over in just a few seconds now.

He allowed himself a backward glance. Just as he had judged, the animal was looming right behind him. He fired himself upwards, as if seeking to escape the terrible trench. He could see a buzzard above him, preparing to strike, convinced he was trying to escape over the top. At the last millisecond, he ground to a halt and immediately plunged back down into the furrow to try and continue his progress.

This action of deceit had worked. The ferret, bigger and, more importantly, much heavier, was unable to check its upward momentum and sailed right over the top, slamming into the slimy mud to the howls of his fellows. Angry, and even more determined, he dived back down after the escaping vole.

This could not last much longer. The frantic pace had nearly ground Vik down. He could now see the end of the furrow but knew he would never reach it. The pursuing animal was so close now he could feel its rapid breath warm on his back. He shot up once more, heading to the edge of the furrow, the animal behind him glued to his tail, his eyes fixed firmly on his quarry. Vik had no intention of escaping. He had spotted a tangle of roots just above him and he dived through with just enough room to spare, but for the larger following ferret there was no way through. In its fervour to catch Vik it had not noticed the bulbous roots ahead of him. Its speed unchecked, it careered into them, knocking itself unconscious to slide to the bottom of the furrow in defeat.

Vik had done it. He was too tired to celebrate. The raucous din had ended, the buzzards and ferrets and weasels shuffling away abjectly, in bad grace grumbling to themselves. Gasping, unable to stand, Vik looked back along the unlovely length, the fox at the other end seemed to be no more than a red dot in the distance. He turned his back on Oswald and Caruthers, growling over his shoulder.

"Go. Never come back." The pair needed no second invitation. They raced over in a matter of seconds to attend and congratulate their exhausted friend. After a short respite the trio were ready to resume their quest, thankfully leaving the large field.

In the next field was a large oak tree. This lonely leviathan grew straight upwards with an umbrella-like canopy of leaves radiating out from its central trunk. Oswald prepared to round the tree. The two birds were relaxing now.

"Phew! That was a close shave! I feel exhausted." Caruthers said to Oswald.

"Yes," Oswald replied, "we'll stop for a little while." Rounding the tree, Oswald's sharp eyes opened wide as he saw him.

Oswald swerved away from the tree. He had no time to call out to his following companion. There, standing perfectly still, was a spotty youth, shotgun at his shoulder. Vik saw him too, though a split second later it seemed to the little vole he was looking down and into two huge tunnels. Then, simultaneously, they lit up, exploding their deadly charge skywards.

BOOM.

Then, an echoing boom, as the sound of the blasting gun reverberated through the nearby woods for which they were heading. Dozens of mini pellets shot at them. Vik could feel a *whoosh* as the pellets lanced through the air. He felt, rather than heard, the owl's dull groan as impact was made, the strength fading from his wings, Oswald trying to gain valuable height. But it was no good. Vik, worriedly looking up at his friend, could feel the warm dark blood speckle his face.

"Oswald! Oswald?" he demanded, in a heartbroken way. The owl remained silent, no longer flying. Just gliding, at a downward angle, the woodland rushing up to meet them. They were already below the treetops, the altitude falling away. Just before they made impact, the owl's talons opened, releasing Vik, the little owl falling to earth to land with a bump on a soft bunch of dandelions, breaking his fall. He rolled over, as if he were a wayward tennis ball.

This was not his wood, his world. Although he was desperate to seek out his friend, Vik had enough animal common sense not to call out.

Without his feathered protector, and the refuge of flight, he felt very small indeed. As the shapes and shadows came into focus, Vik carefully panned around in a three-hundred-and-sixty-degree sweep.

Where was Caruthers? Had he been hit? Was he dead? No sign or sound of the chirpy crow. He moved forward, his little head close to the ground, sniffing, trying to pick up the, by now, familiar scent of the owl. He paused underneath a large, prickly holly bush, resplendent with its autumn crop of bright red berries. Perched a little way above him was a curious Robin, its head cocked to one side inquiringly, puffy chest a blaze of strawberry red. Vik continued his quest, clearing the holly cautiously.

His heart sank with dread as he saw the form beneath him, caked in dirt, covered by leaves and twigs. His friend Oswald's beautiful plumage, stained a dark red wine colour, interspersed with the brown of the muddy woodland floor. Tears welling up, Vik could not control himself. Forgetting about the need to be quiet, he began to cry. He broke down, beaten, inconsolable.

"Oh, oh Oswald!" he lamented.

"Get off! You are standing on my wing, you varmint vole!" Oswald groaned. Vik stopped his wailing in disbelief. A very warm glow of relief and delight was shooting up from his stomach, volcano like.

"You are alive! You are alive!" gasped the vole. Pushing the tears away from his eyes. "I thought you were dead." He managed at last. He did not care if the owl witnessed this display of emotions.

He would not be embarrassed by his show of feelings. The owl was now his best friend, and the feeling of a bond between them was, to Vik, concrete. Slowly, the owl gathered himself up, shaking off the drier blotches of blood with a resurgent flutter of his wings. Still with some concern in his voice, Vik asked the owl as to where he was hit, as to him, it looked like the owl had caught the whole fusillade.

"No," answered Oswald, "a pellet just clipped my wing, and I leaked a small amount of blood."

"What about all that blood on your feathers? And on your chest?"

Oswald looked down at his chest and began to smile. "Oh that, that!" He nodded towards the holly bush standing behind Vik. "I crashed through that holly-bush, and all the red you see covering me isn't blood, just juice from all those berries." Oswald's chest rose up and down as his mirth increased. Vik did not care. He clutched the owls nearest leg and squeezed it as hard as he could, in a gesture of both relief and affection. The owl appreciated this, as he too was aware of the growing value of friendship he shared with the little creature, who never mocked or ridiculed him, just accepted him for what he was.

"No sign of Caruthers?" Oswald inquired of Vik.

"No sign." came the saddened reply. "I did not see him fall or hear him cry out. The blast from the bang-stick was deafening." Lifting his head up to a higher angle, Vik said to Oswald, "Let me see your wing."

The owl dropped his wing so that he could inspect it. Oswald had been right: not much damage, the blood already drying to a darker colour. It was the shock of the attack that had made him slowly faint from the sky. Fluttering up to a safe vantage point, the pair looked from the woodland's canopy, back across to where the ambusher had lain in wait. There was no sign of him, and no sign of Caruthers. Although they knew it could mean danger, the pair took off again to fly past the solitary tree once more, higher this time, just in case, but there was no sign of their comrade. With a heavy heart, the owl and vole made one more sweep, and then continued on their journey to try and rescue Oxy.

Chapter Seven: Under Darkening Trees

Flying as fast as he could, Oswald beat a steady and purposeful path towards the fissure of death, and, if he was still alive, Oxy Mitrus. The morning skies had been invaded by thick, heavy, low cloud, laden with moisture, the wind beginning to pick up. A south-westerly, which would almost certainly mean rain. The unbroken conveyer belt of dark woolly cloud streamed across the countryside, releasing its cargo of water to fall in great sheets of rain, drenching everything in its path. Oswald could feel Vik quivering with cold beneath him, locked securely in his claws.

"Hold on my little friend. I'm going to put you somewhere more sheltered."

"Hhhow?" Vik asked, his teeth chattering together like a piano with its keys being struck at random. There was no answer from the owl. He gained a little more height just in case. Vik could see the ground getting further away. Then, in a manoeuvre a circus acrobat would have been proud of, Oswald launched upwards to nearly vertical, and swung his foot upwards, cannoning Vik into the air, the vole spiralling upwards like a miss-hit rugby ball. No sooner had he done this, the owl turned forward to position himself below the now falling vole. Impeccably judged, the owl felt the rodent land with a bump on his back, felt his feathers tighten as Vik clung on for dear life.

Still in shock, Vik had been too scared to scream. Now holding onto the owl with a firm grip, the vole let rip, shouting and cursing Oswald at the top of his small voice. Oswald said nothing. He had seen the first of the heavy rains rushing to meet them. Instinctively he knew that the vole, with his thin layer of fur, would be chilled to the bone, once he had become soaked. Now, he spoke slowly, with an owl's wisdom.

"Burrow under my feathers, or you'll be in no shape to help your cousin, or me." Just then, the rain struck. Vik wasted no time in doing the owls bidding, reflecting that the owl had only acted with his best interests at heart, guiltily admitting to himself that the owl was a very good friend indeed.

The rain in fact was a double-edged sword, for although it slowed their progress, it also gave them cover. The pair would be harder to spot on this quickly darkening afternoon, the owl lifting now and then to be completely immersed in the billowing, dark puffs. His accuracy unerring, Oswald suddenly changed stroke, pointed his rounded feathered face downward and lost height dramatically.

Vik, ensconced beneath the warm, brown-grey plumage, could feel the air whooshing past just above him as they picked up speed, darting toward the ground. How high they were Vik could not guess, and he certainly was not going to stick his head out into the rushing air. He would have almost surely been ripped from his warm, feathered stronghold. He had had enough wingless flight for one day. Then, as abruptly as he started the decent, Oswald checked his falling flight to level off and glide to earth with all the panache of a drake swan trying to court its mate for the first time.

A slight bump, and touchdown. The owl became motionless, swivelling his head almost completely full circle, as he scanned for danger. Nothing moved, only the sound of rain incessantly drumming on the multitude of leaves covering the woodland floor. Cautiously, Vik emerged from his cockpit of feathers. He did not recognise this wood. To the vole, it seemed a very mournful place. No sparrows chit-chatted back and forth. No insects whirred and clicked. Not even a blackbird's cry of alarm rang out in this desolate wood.

"This is it." whispered Oswald to Vik.

"This is what?" questioned the vole, perplexed.

"This is the Forbidden Forest." Still keeping his voice low, the owl went on, "Once we come to the end of these woods, we will see the Black Chasm." Although he had warmed up, snug underneath his friend's protective blanket, Vik could not help shuddering involuntarily, the shivers telegraphing down his spine, making his tail feel fuzzy, almost like it had lost its circulation.

Looking up at the empty, gnarled branches, Oswald could not see a single nest. The waving boughs slowly moved backwards and forwards in the increasing wind, creaking and moaning as they did so. Although he had never been here before, the owl knew they were in the right place. His father had told him about this place of sorrow, where nothing lived. Not even a fox would meander through the twisted baulks of wood. No badgers set would ever be excavated here, for it would be certain death to trespass. No creatures crossed by land or air.

"What do we do now?" enquired Vik, keeping his voice at a steady level, copying his friend.

"We walk." answered Oswald. Realising that the owl had taken command, knew what to do, Vik obeyed without question, easily keeping up with Oswald. For although he might be graceful as a lark in the air, on the ground he had all the finesse of a drunken sailor, lurching clumsily from step to ungainly step. There was no path to follow, no nature's signpost of the way ahead, for no creature carved a carriageway for them to advance through the untrodden, unbroken undergrowth.

It was slow, arduous going, especially for the owl. Vik nosed through the obstacles with the ease of a butterfly winging its way over a suburban allotment. Ever more menacing, the light began to fade from the sky. The constant beating of the rain disguising the sound of their footsteps, or, in Oswald's case, heavy footsteps.

After what seemed an eternity, the forest, or wood, or whatever else you might call it, began to thin out. More and more mossy ground, with just an odd bush here and there, began to hold sway. The rain began to exhaust itself now, relinquishing control of the clouds to give only a bothersome, intermittent drizzle. Fanned by the wind, Oswald checked his cumbersome momentum to listen intently, though the increasing gusts of wind made it difficult. Straining his magnificent night vision to full stretch, he could pick out the very last tree in the forest: a massive oak. Even this huge woodland leviathan was forced to sway to and fro, like a wreck tossed upon stormy seas.

"Up there," Oswald nodded to Vik, his voice a little louder now, the gusty wind helping to mask his voice somewhat. "We will see how the land lies." He lifted his foot up, talons open. Vik scuttled underneath the talons, which closed softly, the owl making sure he did not injure his friend with his razor-sharp claws. Then, as secure as a miner in a coal pit cage, Oswald whisked Vik aloft, landing on the swaying, giant tree in a matter of seconds. Oswald had made his flight as direct as possible, no wasted flapping around. Again, as before, once he landed he did not move.

"Still now my friend, not a peep." he whispered to Vik,

Sure enough, facing in a northerly direction, was the chalk white escarpment of a limestone cliff, rising from the ground like some medieval sorcerer's castle. Although only forty to thirty feet high, this Hadrian's Wall of limestone was easily the most imposing feature for miles around. Stretching from top to bottom was a great split in the rock, about three metres wide.

This was the black chasm. Trumpetlike, it retreated quite some way, deep into the cliff. Both Oswald and Vik said nothing, carefully panning across the tidal-wave of stone. Oswald could see that the ground just in front of the chasm was covered by what looked like thousands upon thousands of pieces of chalk, like giant peppermints crushed by some unseen ogre's jaws, and then hawked hard at the ground to be discarded. On top of the ridge were huge bushes of once imported rhododendrons, beneath whose foliage nothing could grow.

Now, in early evening's dark cloak, the barn owl waited, trying to devise a plan. The tree they had taken refuge in was about three-hundred metres or so from the entrance to the chasm, and slightly to the right. This was good, for if the wind blew hard enough, as it felt like it should, and blew a clearing in the clouds still scudding overhead, any silhouette given away by the two creatures would, if all went well, be negated by the brilliance of the luminescent full moon; a visual decoy in the sky. Any bored sentries would be looking at the orb of the night, rather than the flight of the incoming would-be rescuers.

The two confederates had no way of knowing if Tremidious and his terrible legions were already encamped in, or around, the coal black, vertical ravine, though Oswald felt it was very early yet, and all things being equal, the ghastly tawny should still be a long way off. Besides, it was known among owl folk that the climax of the night's banqueting, the sacrifice, was usually held at dawn.

How could they reach their goal in secrecy? Trying to wing their way in softly, not having reconnoitred the stronghold, could be suicide. Trying the land approach by tiptoeing on all the small white pieces would be almost impossible. The crunching noise would be like sounding the death knell. Plenty of time yet. Oswald's instincts telling him not to rush, to be cautious, proved to be right. Sensing Vik was finding it difficult to be restrained, to be quiet with a vole's constant high level of activity, Oswald bent down slowly, not making any sudden movement.

"Quiet now Vik. Look at the top of the chasm."

Vik's impatience disappeared immediately. Although his eyesight was nowhere near as good as the owl's pinpoint vision, he too could make out something moving, perhaps fluttering, just at the top part of the mouth of the chasm. A high pitch, staccato chattering broke the early night air, the wind stopping as though nature had closed a giant window. The effect was dramatic. Every sound could now be heard. The high pitch sonic babble was too high in octave for most creatures to hear, especially humans, but the pair could just make out the bottom range of the communicative calls.

Vik looked by Oswald's feet and watched fascinated as a woodlouse trapped on its back waved its legs in an effort to right itself. A strong roll only landed the creature in more trouble. Unable to check its rolling motion, the louse righted itself, lost its footing completely, and fell almost as if in slow motion, soundlessly to the waiting floor below.

Again, that awful high-pitched squealing from the chasm. Oswald, gritting his beak tight shut, hissed to Vik, "Perfectly still. No sound. Radar hunters." As if it were some biblical sea being parted, the clouds above broke rank to allow a large tear in the sky, the full moon's ghostly illumination lighting up the countryside for miles around. Oswald watched, not daring to move, for any vibration, and shuffling on the tree's bough, would be picked up and investigated.

Two huge horseshoe bats slowly and deliberately flapped out of the cabin, scanning the ground beneath them with both their eyes and ears. These were sentries of the chasm, Hermex and Hades. These two ugly and repulsive purveyors of death and misery had long ago scorned the gregarious crowd of their fellow horseshoes, choosing instead to reside in the chasm, in the pay of Tremidious and his cohorts. They had given up their more traditional prey of insects that winged around in the night's sky, much preferring the larder of captured mice, shrews, voles and such like which the owl and his entourage would cheerfully dismember, to be flung mid-air to the bats, the bats seizing the tiny pieces of the hapless rodents to devour them with ghastly relish. No, nowadays a terrified hawk moth that had blundered into their patch was left untouched. They had far bigger, juicier prey to eat.

With departing menace, the two bats faded from sight, busy on their nocturnal rounds of the ghoulish estate. Feeling a little more confident now, Vik said "Shall we try now they are gone?"

"No." said Oswald, concerned that his beating wings give off a vibration that might be picked up by the bat's keen senses. Besides, what if there were more of them waiting up there? "We will walk it. They won't be expecting anything on the ground this late."

"Only a vole with a death wish." said Vik.

"Exactly." said Oswald, his point being proved.

More softly than a hunting housecat stalking a garden finch, they landed, creeping forward, Oswald trying his best to make no noise. Long minutes passed, the pair stopping every now and then to listen for any noise or movement, should the bats swing away from their moonlight patrol and head back to the now silent cliffs.

Vik, his eyesight nowhere near as good in the dark, had caught his foot in one of the bleached little pieces of chalklike rubble. Turning slowly around, Oswald noticed that his pal was lagging behind.

"Keep up Vik! We don't want to be caught out in the open." he hissed.

"My foot's stuck." Came the Vole's quiet reply. Vik reared up, standing on his two back legs, while with his two front paws he tried to free himself from the object which had impeded his progress. Realisation of what it was, what had happened, made him gasp loudly, involuntarily. Discarding the need to be quiet, Oswald retraced his footsteps with two powerful flaps of his wings, concern etched over his feathered features. He bent forward.

"Let me see." Noticing straight away, he too was stunned into a heavy gulp. Both creatures turning around to contemplate what they were standing in, had been travelling through.

"Skulls, Skulls!" moaned Vik.

"Oh no, no!" said Oswald, between sharp intakes of quickly drawn breath. Vik's rear left foot was firmly stuck through the eye socket of some earlier unfortunate victim of the cruel dwellers who lived here. Disbelieving, with a heavy dread, the pair realised what they had observed earlier. It was not broken chalk pieces, but thousands upon thousands of tiny bones. Shattered ribcages, snapped spines and ivory white small rodent and bird skulls. Shaking with fright, small droplets of urine scalding down his small legs, Vik was in grave danger of losing his nerve, freaking out, panicking uncontrollably.

Wilfully forcing himself to regain some of his composure, Oswald quickly grabbed Vik, skull and all, flapping frantically forward towards the chasm. The dark entrance, bathed in eerie moonlight, looked like a huge mouth opening wider and wider. Just as it looked to Vik as if he would be swallowed up, Oswald skimmed across the opening to land, with no finesse, into a small clump of rhododendron bushes, growing on a small rocky precipice about half way up. The smallish, yet dense bushes gave them good cover.

Quickly now, with all the delicacy of a mother pulling a thorn from her child, he closed his foot around the skull and extracted the bony piece from his friend's foot, cleverly rolling it further back into the bush, rather than letting it land back onto the ground below with a sharp crack.

This action was in vain, for the far off, beastly pair of bats' radar was picking up the sounds and relaying it to the command centre of their brains. Wheeling around, they raced back to the direction where the disturbance in the otherwise quiet air had come from. Oswald was doing his best to calm the terrified little vole.

"Vik, Vik!" pleaded the owl. "Quiet now! They will be here any second." Sure enough, the owl's sharp hearing could pick up the returning bat's awful, excited high pitched shrill. Then nothing. Total silence. Oswald dared not move, even closing his eyes, so he could hone his excellent hearing to the maximum. Beneath him, locked in his talons, he could feel Vik quiver spasmodically every now and then.

He became aware, ever so faintly, of a slight scraping to the left of him, and on the same level as he. The owl tried to breathe as shallowly as he could. The suspense he felt, must surely be visible. He felt it leaping from him, as if he were a volcano spewing out red hot lava. The scratching, shuffling sounds came ever nearer. Then he saw it, one of the giant horseshoes was no more than a metre from them, sniffing the cool, damp night air, he was straining to pick up a sound; any sound. Eyes were straining forward, trying to pierce the gloom of their leafy rhododendron sanctuary.

From behind the owl, completely surprising him, came "I told you there's nothing there. Probably a small twig falling from above the cliff and landing on the floor." It was the other bat, so close he would surely see the frozen, immobile pair. Vik and Oswald could feel the hot, fetid breath on their backs. Launching silently in unison, the bats flapped back up to their vantage point, to finish their freshly caught treat: a hapless baby mole, an unexpected and delightful delicacy. Still Oswald and Vik did not move. They could hear the bats conversing above them.

"What time will the master be here?"

"After midnight I should think, when the moon is much higher." said the other, crunching a thighbone as if it were a cornflake. Gradually, silence returned to the cliff, the two bats lapsing into a fitful sleep.

Chapter Eight: The Dictator's Parliament

Able to relax at last, Oswald and Vik stretched their stiff limbs, or wings, in the owl's case. Gradually, their circulation returned after their forced paralysis. Gently pressing his face to Vik's ear, the owl whispered to him.

"Time to go now my friend. Have a look inside." Vik felt his friend's claws lock solidly around him, and with a minimum of effort, virtually without noise, Oswald glided from their bushy refuge. Not so much as brushing a leaf, gliding down to floor level, Oswald coasted into the chasm.

Here it was very dark, though not as black as the pair had expected. There were two or three gashes in the ceiling of the creepy cavern, where the constant leeching of rainwater had eaten away through the rock. Vik was relieved to hear the water splattering onto the floor of the cave, blotting out most sounds, unless exceptionally loud. He knew this would give them some protection from the sleeping sentinels at the chasm's entrance.

Slowly at first, their eyes became accustomed to this darker place. Placed at strategic points were large nests of twigs, hay, pieces of bark and so on. Confident now that the falling water would muffle his wings' powerful strokes, Oswald took flight again, climbing to a perch, one foot grabbing the edge of the nest, the other clutching Vik tightly. The nest was empty, though looking down, the pair could see that it had been comfortably lined with feathers, soft leaves and, more disturbingly, fur of some sort.

"Weesh! This place gives me the creeps." Vik whispered. Oswald hooted quietly in agreement. This was indeed an unlovely place. The air was heavy with moisture, a cold, chilling damp that penetrated protective fur or feather, eating away at the warmth inside. Oswald hopped off his perch and into the nest, surprisingly deep. Only when he stood bolt upright could the owl clearly see over the rim of the nest. This better vantage point gave them a panoramic view of Tremidious' lair.

The floor was carpeted by ream upon ream of ghostly white toadstools, growing with relish in this moist, dark, cool climate. To the barn owl they looked like dozens upon dozens of small children's upturned faces, reminding him of one day that his secretive daylight search for fruit and berries had taken him across an infants' school playground. The children, noticing the strange looking bird, tilting their small faces upwards to obtain a better view, their far off excited chatter wafting up to him like the smoke from a garden's winter bonfire. Delighted at the attention, he had indulged himself, showing off his repertoire of airborne stunts until he had hit the telegraph wire.

A whispered question from Vik jerked him out of his little daydream.

"I said," repeated Vik, "what now?"

"Hang on," answered the owl, Oswald carefully scanning the floor, the empty nests, for Vik's cousin. No cage could he find, no stake with a poor rodent tethered to it. Where was he? Surely, they could not have missed this sorrow ceremony of Oxy Mitris death.

"We wait," Oswald went on. "There's no sign of him Vik."

Down in the bowls of the nest, Vik gulped. So that was it then. They would have to wait for the killer flock to return. Vik had been nursing the secretive hope that they would find Oxy quickly, and be on their way, making their dash for freedom over and away from the Forbidden Forest. He steeled himself in the realisation that this was not going to be possible. Nothing for it then. They would just have to wait.

The hours dragged slowly past, the moon drooping from its high arc in the sky to fall over and away from the chasm's entrance now. Its penetrating light bored through the gaps in the chasm's roof to illuminate it quite spectacularly. The beams of light reminded Vik of the great marble columns used to support buildings of heritage and great importance; not that Vik had ever seen one, though he had heard them described to him by a family of city sewer rats he had once met, while they made their way to holiday at a fast food outlet in a nearby town. They would then pass on for a quieter life on a new housing estate that they had heard was being built on the rat grapevine.

"Plenty of workman's sandwiches and pasties there, my old son." Had proclaimed the chief rat and navigator of the rodent ramblings.

Still no sign of any activities, time dragging on as slowly as a lawnmower drags across the cricket green on a sunny afternoon. His eyes becoming heavy, the vole felt himself drifting slowly into sleep, his head nodding forward then jerking back suddenly as his battle to keep awake repeated again. Then at last they heard it. A series of *twit-twit* owl cries, with the power of many voices pitched together. Oswald did not look down at his friend. Instead he stared hard at the mouth of the chasm, uttering the words, "They are coming."

Tiny cold spasms of fear played across Vik's back, bitter as a Siberian Winter wind. There could be no going back now. The shrill owls' cries were building, getting louder, waking the two sleeping bats guarding the mouth of the chasm. They replied to their master's escorts' enquiring call with their own cacophony of sound.

Vik continued to tremble every now and then. Oswald sank slowly deeper into the nest. The noise now was almost deafening, disorientating the way it whirled around and bounced off the limestone walls. No covert approach to the chasm. Tremidious was top dog of the skies around here. Even a wayward, belligerent buzzard would be quickly seen off by his minions in no uncertain manner; such was the owl and his followers' confidence that they would make as much noise as possible as they travelled to the far outposts of the cruel owl king's domain. The screeching bedlam served to cow and terrify the other creatures of the fields and woodlands into continuing their fear riven subservience.

Heavy fluttering at the entrance now. Bursting into view, a huge owl led his feathered followers inside, the noise now seeming so loud it would blow the entire rocky roof off their den. Oswald watched through half closed eyelids as Tremidious flew straight past, heading for the darker depths at the back of the cavern. He truly was a massive owl. Oswald had never seen anything as big. Even his bodyguards, carefully guarding the three female owls brought to enjoy the spectacles, were the size of large seagulls usually to be found at the town's far off refuse tip.

The entourage alighted on the nests carefully spaced around Tremidious' throne of soft, fresh green ferns. They ceased their excited screeching almost as one when the emperor owl gave them a commanding look.

The throne he had taken residence on was more like a swan's nest, usually found on a lake. Oswald had been right not to harbour there; his caution justified. Another look from the super-sized tawny and the three young females joined him in his giant nest with owl-like obsequiousness. Tremidious jerked his head back and roared.

"Food!" The command reverberated off the walls louder than an artillery salvo. A short pause and the two bats entered through the roof, a hapless array of entangled mice, shrews and a couple of juicy dormice added for good measure dangled from the bats' claws, trapped in what looked to be thin pieces of stripped elm bark, or similar. The terrified rodents' piteous pleading to be released only increased from the look of pleasure on Tremidious' face.

Vik, having carefully joined Oswald in peering over the lip of their refuge, could see the owl's features defined in the weakening moonlight. Two huge, piercing, saucer like eyes dominated the face. A beak as big and powerful as a claw hammer. A heavy brow, the scars of many a battle for dominance, always won, crisscrossing the owl's face.

"You first, my beauties." Tremidious grudgingly growled. Just as the king's owls, the three horrible harpies, were about to rip into the offering of writhing, enmeshed rodents the bats had dutifully dropped into the oversized nest, the powerful owl reversed his command.

"Stop. Wait. Where is the strange creature that was caught yesterday? Show me. Let me see him." he ordered.

Tremidious was not in the least bit hungry. He rarely hunted himself these days, offerings of homage, some dead, some alive, were brought to him by a stream of owls currying favour, hoping to be accepted in his powerful court. The two bats hanging upside-down, near the evil owl, took off in agitated obedience, vanishing out through the roof the way they had come in. Vik, watching and listening intently, could not help rearing up in anticipation and relief that he would soon clap eyes on his cousin once more.

"Careful! Not too high. If they see us at this stage, its curtains." Oswald whispered. Curtains it certainly would be, especially for the owl. There would be short shrift for the feathered turncoat, consorting with their food and the playthings of this airborne Caesar and his legion. Death would not be swift, but it would certainly be awful. Oswald, remembering this, gulped painfully. A short pause, and the bats dropped back into the now returning gloom, the moon sinking beyond the horizon, dawn almost ready to answer nature's curtain call.

"Over here! Bring it over here!" The two bats obeyed nervously. Not even they felt comfortable being so near the terrible tyrant. As delicate as a jeweller examining a valuable gem, they placed Oxy on the open edge of the nest, for if he should die now – his heart give out, for instance – the consequences would be terrible for them. Heavily, with the powerful muscles in his legs bulging, Tremidious moved forwards towards the terrified Oxy, near faint with fear. A few long seconds ticked by as the huge owl decided Vik's cousin's fate. Then at last, he spoke.

"He is large for a rodent. Plenty of meat on him!" His eyes fluttered as a thought dawned on him. "Yes," Tremidious thought out loud. "Yes, we will play swipe with him. You will enjoy this." he said to the three enraptured females by his side. Tilting his head back to roar powerfully once more, he commanded, "Take him to the roof. Secure him." A pause, then he went on, "the one leg only."

This would make the hideous fate about to befall Oxy go on all the longer, coax a little bit more pain, more terror from the pitiful creature, already half dead with fear. To tie Oxy was the job of the two bats. Their nimble claws could tie the length of stripped ivy twine around Oxy's leg, then connect it to a root working its way down through the cave's roof. There was no way an owl could do this; their claws too heavy for this nimble work. Neither could they nearly hover, hold station like the bats. This was one of their specialities, one of the reasons they were allowed to live unmolested to prosper in the chasm's regular bloody carnage.

To Vik, slyly looking up, it looked like his cousin had been tethered to the roof of the world, so high was he. Oswald's keen eyesight had picked out four or five similar methods of imprisonment. Hanging listlessly down were the leg or tail of previous unfortunates, rotting now. Proof of the hideous death: no escape.

"Let it go!" screeched Tremidious. The bats holding station way above released Oxy immediately, the terrified animal shrieking with unbridled fear as he plunged straight down. The coils of the twine straightened out, unable to pay out any more length, and he was suddenly jerked back upwards, as if on a giant bungee cord. Such was the jolt; his tethered leg broke with an audible crack, the little animal screaming out in anguish and agony. A cheer broke out from the watching owls and Tremidious roared his approval of the wail of pain breaking out above him. "Let the game begin!" he bellowed.

Described briefly, 'Swipe' simply meant that Oxy would be shoved every now and then by the two bats positioning themselves mid-air either side of Oxy. The force of their contact would send him spiralling around and around, but more importantly, sent him swinging across the chasm in a wide unpredictable arc. As this happened, the owls would launch off their perches, swoop by the gyrating prisoner, and slash at him, with their sabre sharp talons, or try to rip pieces off the poor victim with their cleaver like beaks.

This was a great way for an up and coming young owl to prove himself, to show his aerial skill off to Tremidious and his lieutenants. A forelimb ripped off would immediately be whisked down to the king's throne to be offered at his feet. This would carry great admiration among the feathered court if done properly. On the other hand, if a too eager young owl mistimed his vicious and enthusiastic young swipe and disembowelled the helpless captive, bringing the game to a premature end, he would be mocked and laughed at, but not much else. After all, there were plenty more that could take the unfortunate little creature's place.

"Who will be first?" questioned Javelin, Tremidious' malicious master at arms. He was so named for the way he would fly straight and true at any prey or dissenter of the owl leader. He never bothered to use his claws. He would jerk his head back with consummate timing, then at the last second, he would bring it forward to impale his opponent with his powerful beak, rupturing its internal organs with shattering force. In his own mind, competitors should be the owls that had proved themselves to Tremidious with their courage, loyalty and savagery, not some half grown fledgling, still warm from his mother's nest.

He would grimace as the young owls, learning their trade in torture, would clumsily bump into the tethered victims, sometimes missing altogether.

The chasm river reverberated to the excited hoots and shrieks of the young owls as they jostled and vied with each other to be first. Javelin cocked his head over to one side, looking over at his raptor ruler to see who would be chosen. Slowly, scanning the highly excited young owls jostling underneath him, Tremidious made his decision.

"You there." He had picked out an ungainly looking owl, perched precariously on the edge of one of the nests. The young predator looked overweight, heavy as if he had too many offerings from his mother, rather than the calorie burning coursing of the chase itself. Tremendously honoured to be chosen first, the owl looked around at his fellow lower ranks. He puffed his chest out and dove forward and down to pick up speed. Having done this, and trying to impress the watching and waiting spectators, he launched upwards in a near vertical manoeuvre.

Unfortunately for him, his idea of a rapier, jet like strike was more reminiscent of a clumsy old bi-plane. Missing his target completely, made worse by the fact that as he desperately twisted around to try and locate his intended victim, he was dealt a smack on the back of his head by the swinging rodent. Flaking in embarrassment, he half flew, half flopped down to his original position, head bowed low as a deluge of derision and laughter rained down on him.

The more senior owls had hoped this would happen. The youngsters below them were so keen, so full of eagerness to attack the inverted creature that they invariably missed on the first one or two attempts. The older owls split their sides in cruel, mocking laughter. The young owl, a tawny who went by the name of Farrow, was deeply upset and embarrassed. Luckily for him, his great coat of glossy feathers hid his burning red skin underneath. It would be somebody else now. Perhaps they would come a cropper like he had. The young overweight owl hoped it fervently. Again, a long penetrating stare from Tremidious, then motioning with one of his huge wings.

"You, up there, on your own. You're next."

Chapter Nine: Vegetarian Swipe

He had tried to cover, to back down into the nest, but too late. Oswald had been spotted by the aerial Tartar. With the speed of light, he shot out of the nest, a foot closing around Vik.

"Sire, I have caught a prisoner already." Oswald bleated nervously, trying in vain to make his voice sound strong, confident, at ease with the evil proceedings going on around him. This last was a mistake. Nobody ever questioned Tremidious, nor dared not do his bidding immediately. The excited babbling of the highly charged young owls, the laughter of the more senior, elder birds, even the incessant chattering of the two bats curtailed and died off at once. A fork of lightning could not have silenced them more quickly. This was unheard of. Dare to question the leader? Tremidious was unable to speak, such was his disbelief at not meeting total subservience from one of his kind. Before his composure had returned, Javelin had taken flight, anticipating his master's command.

"Seize him! Capture that upstart now!" raged the king.

Oswald was petrified, the sight of Javelin hurtling towards him seemed to transfix him. He simply could not move. Vik, knowing that they only had seconds left, broke through Oswald's immobilising fear. He nipped the owl hard.

"Come on Oswald, its now or never!" he screamed. Galvanised into action at last, the shock, the mesmerising sight of the powerful owl bearing up at them, Oswald flipped back over to land on the nest once again, as if exhausted, the towel thrown in. Then, at the very last moment, with perfect timing, he rocketed airborne once more. Javelin, arrowing through the air with the speed of a dart, his much greater weight telling, was unable to halt of change direction. Crashing face first into the nest with a heavy impact, the nest exploding with a force sending shards of twigs and leaves in every direction.

It was the squadrons of owls' turn to be frozen in immobility now. Javelin NEVER missed. Yet, in front of their very eyes, Tremidious' trusted wingman was floundering, dazed on the cold damp floor of the cavern. His wings flapping furiously, Oswald continued his upward progress, heading straight for Oxy. The watching owls were not sure what to make of this strange new young owl that had first queried their king, then had made a fool out of Javelin, yet was now obeying Tremidious' original order, or so they thought.

Knowing that he only had one attempt at this, and not wanting to damage Oxy any further, Oswald turned his head, now level with the wildly swinging rodent. He snapped with his beak at the twine ensnared mouse, the vine shearing instantly in a perfectly timed manoeuvre. He rolled over onto his side and, with all the panache of a test cricket fielder, closed his one empty remaining claw on the fallen, and by now unconscious, Oxy. His claw locked on more securely than a Venus Flytrap. He was not going to drop the New World visitor now, no way.

Coming out of their trance, the watching owls gasped in grudging admiration at this airborne artistry, for very few owls managed to make a manoeuvre like this at the very first attempt. A chorus of "Oooh" and "ahhh!" resounded around the chasm, now slowly lighting up as the breaking dawn's fingers of early daylight began to probe Tremidious' lair. Half placated, Tremidious watched as Oswald slowed, his speed reduced by the cargo held in his undercarriage.

The king of owls' beak dropping in disbelief, he watched as Oswald banked around, inches away from the royal nest, and dived down into the now well-lit chasm. Such was his control on his fellows, his complete mastery, that he simply could not bring himself to realise what was going on. His eyes had taken in the information but his brain, for now, was unable to process it. Where the owl and his twin cache of rodents should be, there was only empty space. Save from the sounds of Javelin groggily reviving, the chasm was deathly quiet.

Tremidious gasped, first in horror, then volcanic fury.

"Get them! Kill them! Now, all of you!" Needing no second bidding, though still taking off in near stunned disbelief, the owls streaked out of the chasm and into the quickly strengthening sunlight. Sharp eyes scanned in every direction, acute ears were turned this way and that to pick up any sound that the escaping trio might make. The impudent death wish rescuer had simply vanished. Tremidious circled above the entrance to the chasm, quivering with fury, at last joined by a fully composed Javelin. He knew that if his followers saw this liberty being taken, other aspiring leaders might make a play for his throne: a feathered rebellion. There would have to be swift, and very cruel, retribution.

"Any sign?" he asked.

"No sire." His number two angrily conceded.

His mind racing, Tremidious thought for a moment, then said, "Bring out those two bats."

"Straight away sire." Responded Javelin.

"But they won't fly in daylight sire." one of the elder owls said. The owl chieftain slowly turned his head, menacingly, towards the speaker.

"Tell them that if they don't come out to me, I will fly into them, and tear their wings off. Slowly.

They can then spend the rest of their days crawling on the floor, hoping that they don't get eaten by a weasel, or devoured by a stoat. Well don't just float there, get on with it!"

"Yes sire, yes sire!" said the owl, disappearing back down into the chasm's entrance.

Landing on the top of a small tree, Tremidious now outlined his battle plan to the two squinting bats, uncomfortable in the sunlight. They were to fly in ever-widening circles and use their gift of radar to locate the fleeing friends. He then managed to hang on to his white-hot temper.

To emphasise the point, he went on "Failure will not be accepted." He added "Come back without them..." He had made his point. Each bat began radiating away from the cliffs, a platoon of owls keeping station behind them, watching intently for their signal, a sign of contact.

The fleeing trio were making slow progress. Weakened by the last few day's exertions and not enjoying the fulfilling nourishment that his fellow meat-eating owl brethren enjoyed, Oswald was nowhere near the strong swift near silent aviator of the dusk skies that Vik had first encountered.

"Hold on dear friend, nearly there." whispered Vik, looking up at the courageous creature.

Heartened by this, Oswald redoubled his efforts to keep flying, to put as much distance between them and Tremidious' ferocious followers who he felt must surely be frantically looking for them.

They had re-entered the forbidden forest, trying to keep as straight a flying line as possible, though this was made difficult by the interwoven branches of silent trees, never bothered by a woodpecker's persistent drumming, or a marauding squirrel, intent on stripping their bark. Not even in summer time did any of the leaf eating insects that abound in other forests or woods dare to enter here. Springtime here was a silent affair, the flora and fauna on the forest floor interlocking like nature's giant jig-saw. The only sure-fire way to pass through here quickly was to fly above it, though no creature ever did, as death waited patiently in the sky above.

"I have got to rest Vik!" gasped Oswald.

"For a little while." said Vik, calculating that they were half way through the forest. He knew they should continue, but he could see, hear and sense that his good friend, his cousin's saviour, was beat.

"Ok," Vik agreed, trying to sound positive, "put down on that tree right in front of us." Oswald landed awkwardly, nearly tipping over and losing his balance, unable to grasp the branch with his sharp talons, as they both held the precious cargo of the two little rodents. Once his momentum was checked, Oswald released Vik, who straight away scampered round to check on his unconscious cousin.

As softly as he dared, Vik whispered, "Oxy, Oxy?" The little South American stirred slightly but did not open his eyes.

"Is he ok?" asked Oswald with concern etched across his feathered brow.

"He is still unconscious," murmured Vik, instinct telling him to keep is voice low. Vik went on, "He needs water. No point looking after him if they only intended keeping him alive for a day or so." said the grim-faced vole. The sun was much higher in the sky now, filtering its warmth through the scaffolding of intertwining growth. Vik began to feel a little safer. Surely Tremidious and his henchman would be put off the hunt now, especially in broad daylight and in this wood, even if they had happened to have flown in the right direction.

An hour or so passed, and Oswald began to recover some of his bloom, their spirits rising with the temperature. Even Oxy snuffled once weakly. Sensing Vik's question, Oswald answered "I am ready."

"Ok, good." Replied Vik, carefully, looking around, listening intently. No sign of life, no sign of danger. Hard to believe that there was no life in this woodland desert.

Looking forward to plan their flight, Oswald said to Vik "Did we come this way? I can't see our way through that lot." He nodded his head at the trees in front of him, forming into an impenetrable fortress of branches. Vik knew his pal was right. It would take all day to fly, weave and crawl through the daunting tangle in front of them. It certainly did not look like the way they had come on their cautious route to the chasm. The plucky little vole made his decision.

"We will go over the top. Make a run for it." To Oswald, this seemed like a good idea. The thermals that would be building on this windless day would not be as strong as on a hot summer's evening but would still give a welcome assist to the tired owl's wings. They took off in lumbering fashion, knowing that once they had cleared the forest, safety would be waiting with open arms.

"Well?" demanded Javelin for the umpteenth time.

"Nothing." answered Hades timidly. He was about to ask Javelin if they could take a break. They had seemed to be airborne for hours and the sunlight was painful to his nocturnal eyes. Suddenly he felt it. *Blip, blip, blip*. He held his breath, scarcely daring to believe that his luck may have turned, for he was under no illusion as to what would happen to himself and Hermex should they return empty handed without the escapees. Again, he felt it: *blip, blip, blip.* His brain, honed by millions of years of finding his prey by this means of sending out a signal and interpreting the reply, slipped into gear.

"Contact! Contact!" said Hades, in a beastly, bat sort of way.

"Where? Where?" Javelin barked, his huge hooked beak only millimetres away from the cowering yet excited bat.

"To the South to the South! Going away from us. The signal is getting fainter."

As fast as lightning, Javelin barked out his orders. "Climb on my back. You will fly too slowly and we will lose them." He snapped tersely to one of the younger owls keeping station behind them. "You. Go and tell Tremidious that we have found them and are following. Make sure you bring the other bat so that you can track us. I'm sure the king will want to punish that upstart for himself. Well don't just flap there, get on with it! The rest of you, follow me."

A bursting chorus of excited hoots and shrieks of approval erupted from the waiting squadron of owls around him. What a day. A chance to fly in daylight. Tremidious usually strictly forbid it. Now though, with the chance to be involved in the airborne hunt, glory would surely go to the one who caught this rogue owl. Recognition from Tremidious, if not a gracious promotion. Maybe even, perhaps, a chance to sit on his council. The owls' imaginations ran riot as they chased after Javelin and the terrified bat, who was clinging on for dear life.

Guiding them, Javelin knew that if he verbally ravaged the frightened bat any more, the escapee owl would be gone for good. He managed to control himself with great effort, his frustration mounting. Hades had already fainted once; it must not happen again.

The younger of the two bats could only mutter his replies incoherently to Javelin's persistent demands as to how much further and how long. It was the same for Hermex. Such was his fear, he could feel his stomach burning in panic as he desperately fired out signal after signal to try and locate the fleeing trio.

Then, thank heavens, "There sire, over there!" Tremidious rotated his powerful head and spied the young owl racing across the white sea of small rodent bones to meet them.

"What news?" Tremidious asked with authority, knowing that he would have to wait a few seconds while the excited youngster calmed down and could get his breath back. In between great gasping lungful's of air, the juvenile bird relayed the information that Javelin had entrusted to him.

"Lord Javelin says to come as quickly as possible, your grace. They have set after them and hope to close on them before nightfall."

"Well done." Tremidious replied curtly. Turning around to one of the sleeker birds, he ordered, "Take this hopeless horseshoe on your back." Narrowing his eyes, he growled at Hermex, "Lose track of my lieutenant and today will be your last. Is that clear?"

"Oh y-y-y-yes your m-majesty." grizzled the miserable bat.

Taking in a deep breath, the king of owls let out a roar, "We move now, full speed!" Again, a chorus of vengeful consent from the phalanx of birds keeping station behind their cruel king.

Chapter Ten: Pursuit in the Skies

Vole, rat and owl broke from the cover of the treetops, the warm air giving Oswald's tired wings some ease. It was make or break, now or never. Free from having to negotiate the twisted flight through the branches below, they were making good time. It was as if the rapidly rising sun was taking their spirits with it, higher and higher. Both Vik and Oswald began to relax just a little bit.

"Not much further now and we should see the end of this cursed place, and then be safe." said Oswald. His wings seeming to become stronger, now that they had their goal almost in sight.

"Thank goodness!" answered Vik below him. "This is one adventure I definitely do not care to repeat."

They both saw it at the same time. At last, the rippled edge of the ghostly forest below them was coming into sight. Beyond it, broken rolling countryside, then the ordered fields of agriculture beginning to hold sway. The duo, cheering up even more now, excited and with great relief, were chattering back and forth to each other.

"When Oxy recovers, we will take him on a tour of the greenhouse's gorgeous grapes." chirped Vik gleefully.

"I hope that cat's not there waiting!" Both broke out into great peals of laughter as they recalled the way the old gardener had propelled the hapless feline with his boot into the bushes and shrubs surrounding the glass palace of sweet fruit and vines.

"At last!" sighed Vik, "Some friendly faces." Rising up, just some way off the forest, Oswald could see what Vik meant. A gaggle of what looked like ducks, at this distance, flapped slowly across their path, wings beating up and then downward in unison with an unhurried stroke.

"Oh boy am I glad to see them!" gushed Oswald. "We made it Vik, we made it! Am I tired, I think I will sleep for a week!" he looked down at his friend. He was about to look away when he noticed that Vik's expression of happiness and relief had begun to change. Puzzlement was now starting to etch itself across his face.

"They've changed direction," Vik said, "and their wing beat is different."

Oswald looked up and away from the vole. A stab of naked fear slashed at his heart. He knew instantly by the stroke what they were. Owls. Lots of them. Both Vik and Oswald were stunned, their hope escaping from them. His heartbeat rising markedly, Vik was first to grasp his wits.

"Turn Oswald, for pity's sake!" Oswald turned slowly, hypnotised by the sight of the owls now fanning out behind them, set to engulf them the same way a trawl-net closes on a doomed shoal of fish.

"Flap! Fly faster, quickly now my friend!" At last the owl woke from his trance, working his wings up and down for all he was worth, nosing down slightly to pick up more speed and put vital space between them and their pursuers. Vik, with difficulty, managed to turn himself on his back. He could now lift his head up slightly and gauge the situation.

Events had taken an awful turn for the worst. They were being driven back into the forests' hinterland, away from the tantalisingly close safety of the edge of the trees flashing past beneath them. With skilful hunter's precision the chasing owls drew nearer. Fresh young wings, unladen with any dead weight, more than a match for the tired Oswald, fanned out behind them and to their right.

They slowly turned the courageous pair through a half-circle, coursing them into the direction that they wanted. Vik, looking back, could see their determined pursuers closing as they came much nearer now. He could make out Javelin, a deathly grin of pleasure on his face, anticipating with lurid glee what was to come.

Come it did, but not from the direction that they expected.

As Oswald tried in vain to extricate himself and his two charges from their perilous position, he veered sharply to the left, then quickly back to the right. He shot a glance backward; the manoeuvre had worked but not as well as he had hoped. Two of the larger owls had collided, panicking they spiralled down to the waiting forest below. Oswald had hoped to take more than two out of commission with his aerobatics.

Seeing that his increasingly desperate strategy was not going to work, knowing there was no way he could outrun his terrible trackers, he spotted a large clearing opening out beneath them. He nosed vertically over, frantic in his efforts to escape Javelin and his subordinates. Facing backwards, Vik twisted around in Oswald's claw to face down and front again. He saw him too late. Oswald did not see him at all.

Rising like a rocket beneath them was Tremidious. There was no time to cry out to his friend, to scream or utter a warning. There was a terrible crash, thunder like, then for a brief second, everything went black. Just as swiftly, the light returned again. It was Oswald's turn to hurtle to earth now.

Vik could tell by the uncontrolled way that they were falling that Oswald had been badly hurt.

He could see both of his friend's great wings bent backwards by the force of the air they were rushing through. Even more alarming was the scarlet spew of blood, streaking out from the owl as the stricken bird plummeted down towards the forest. The tops of the trees were very close now. What had fate in store for them? A quick demise as they were impaled by the sharp upper branches, or an even quicker *splat*, then oblivion, as they slammed into the hard, unyielding floor of the clearing?

A hard, jarring sensation was followed by an awful cracking, spluttering sound, as they ripped high speed through the cold forest's canopy. Vik's eyes were squeezed tightly shut. He hoped against hope that, should he live through this hellish decent, he would still have managed to save his sight.

Another heavy impact and he was wrenched from the unconscious Oswald's grip. He felt himself cartwheel through the air to land miraculously with a bump on a mound of soft, moist earth just on the edge of the clearing, the earth made all the softer by the colony of ants residing underneath it. It was this ant's nest that had saved him, though for a moment he was too weak and disorientated to notice. The young vole felt his heart pounding at a ridiculously fast rate. He felt himself mercifully slipping into unconsciousness as the effects of the shock of the fall to earth began to take hold.

Tremidious had alighted on the highest branch of the tallest tree with a great sense of satisfaction. He looked down at the motionless owl. His plan had worked perfectly, Javelin and his squad had done exactly as they'd been ordered. They had driven Oxy's desperate rescuers away from the safety of the forest border, then skilfully spearheaded them straight into Tremidious' waiting wings.

He had spotted them a long way off, frantically trying to avoid capture from his dutiful lieutenant. The king of owls had deployed his troops in such a way that should he have mistimed his upwards strike on the traitorous owl, then his vengeful disciples would have closed on Oswald from every direction. He had even managed to keep quiet that incessant squealing bat. He had struck this lightweight jockey hard with his anvil of a beak, knocking him out cold. He could not have him shrieking their position underneath the escapers at the last moment.

He had felt with no small relish his sharp claws rip through Oswald's feathers at high speed, magnified by the two animals closing upon each other. He had not really had to do anything; the momentum had done the damage. A grin of cruel pleasure on his face, he could still feel the feathers giving way to flesh, and the flesh to bone, cutting out deep furrows through Oswald's chest. If the owl was not dead, well he ought to be.

Aware that an audience had settled around him, and respectfully beneath him, the excited hunters' chatter at last gave way to silent obedience.

"This is what happens when there is disobedience, and we do not stick together. Divided we are weak. We do not see things the way lesser creatures do." Tremidious went on, "Voles, mice, smaller creatures, they are our prey. Our playthings. They exist only to serve our needs. Stray from my rule and, well…" a heavy pause as he let his words take effect, then continued, "you can see the results of rebellion beneath you."

He raised himself to his full height and was about to carry on when one of the young minions interrupted excitedly.

"Sire, he lives, he moves!" Looking down, the feathered Tsar could see that the sharp eyed young owl was right. Oswald moved once or twice on the forest floor, weakly, spasmodically. That was it. He would show his followers one final lesson in retribution.

"Follow me," he ordered, as he moved forward into flight, heading straight for the stricken bird. He landed on the forest's tangled covering of twigs and leaves. Walking on the floor is not easy for an owl, but Tremidious managed it with some difficulty. Surrounding him were the audience of expectant owls. Gleefully, and with rising excitement, they waited for their king to rip to shreds the badly injured Oswald, wagering what the king would do to dispatch him. His beak? His talons? The atmosphere was reaching fever pitch.

"Stand him up. Revive him." he commanded. He was determined to make an example of this owl. "I will give him a fair chance," Tremidious proclaimed. "A fight to the death. If he should win, then his freedom is granted. If he should lose," a burst of cackles and mocking laughter. The badly injured owl win? Impossible. Then, the large, powerful owl said, "Find and bring that vole to me. He can watch his friend die."

A few long minutes had passed, and Oswald had regained consciousness. He felt terribly weak. Looking down, he could see the deep incisions cut into his chest, could feel the warm blood still slowly oozing out from it, and knew that he had but one chance. Unable to stand properly, he was held up by his two wings, outstretched to stabilise him, two owls holding each of his wings in their beaks, neither taking care to be gentle. Although exhausted, he still had an owl's natural cunning. As he swayed back and fore, he could hear Tremidious' voice, but could not understand it. He knew what was expected. He was to die, gladiatorial fashion.

He knew that Tremidious would put on a show of his death, his entrails strewn around the clearing, his organs would be tossed jubilantly through the air in a demonic ritual of barbarism. He watched helplessly as Vik was retrieved from farther into the forest, Javelin slowly closing his beak on Vik's ear. The blood began to spurt, dragging him from his shocked slumber with an alarm call of pain.

The owls spread out, forming a circle around their king and Oswald. Oswald could see no pity in their eyes, only cruel, savage anticipation. Well he would not give them a spectacle. He would not fight a fight he had no chance of winning. No show of combat would they get from he. His strategy slowly dawned on him. As soon as he was released from the two demons holding his wings in a captive embrace he would steel himself against his pain.

Vik watched from across the clearing. His ear felt terrible. Great waves of pain shot through him. He felt sick, faint, could feel his blood, his life's warm liquid, leaking away from him. He knew that this was his and Oswald's last roll of the dice. He could see Oswald dizzily looking at him.

"Thank you." he murmured with heartfelt gratification, for the owl had risked everything to help him. He had gone against his own kind, his own family, and would now pay with his life. There, savouring every second of misery, and basking in his own self-importance, Tremidious opened his beak to order Oswald's release. He was going to roar "Let battle commence!" or maybe "To the death!"

In the event, he said neither.

Chapter Eleven: Feathered Revolution

A cacophony of *cawcaus* and howls broke the expectant silence within the still forest with all the force of a bomb. Any bird's instinct when alarmed is to take flight, as one of the owls launched into the air in ambushed disarray. Above the owls, the air was darkened by more and more attacking crows. Dozens and dozens became hundreds and hundreds, plunging down towards the owls trapped below them in sheer panic. Suicidal in their fury, the crows slammed head on, again and again, into the fearful owls.

One to one, an owl is more than a match for a crow, but in these narrow woodland confines speed, agility and surprise were too much for the cumbersome followers of the owl king. They were being overwhelmed and outnumbered in a series of brutal, bloody, sprawling dogfights.

Panic set in as the owls exploded outwards, trying to find some sort of sanctuary in the thick tangle of branches and bushes that surrounded the clearing. Here again, it was the smaller, faster attacking birds that held sway, as one by one, the owls were covered in a writhing mass of angry, shiny black carrion birds and were driven relentlessly to the floor, ferociously pecked and clawed into submission.

Almost as stunned as his captors, Oswald could see the chance of escape staring him in the face, forcing his tired and sore wings yet again into action. He lifted forward into flight, trying to pick up speed as quickly as he could, his wings beating frantically. He covered the clearing in a trice, heading straight for the log onto which Vik had been held captive. He circled tightly around, looking desperately for his friend. Somehow, miraculously above the din, he heard Vik's familiar voice.

"Up here Oswald, up here!" He looked up. Directly above him was the vole, held in a painful grip by Javelin. Vik's captor was ferociously battling with a trio of aggressive, determined crows. Changing the angle of his wings to give him more lift, Oswald accelerated upwards, towards the mid-air melee. When he judged he was level he banked over, heading straight at the embattled owl. Mustering all his speed, he cannoned into Javelin, knocking the wind from him with a loud, painful gasp. The impact had the desired effect. The jolt, the shock of the collision, had made the bird involuntarily open his talons. Vik, no longer restrained, was hurtling through the air downwards. Oswald plunged after him, a desperate lunge, just managing to save his friend from being impaled on a sharp hazel twig.

"Gotcha!" said Oswald, in a joyous tone.

"Am I glad to see you!" said Vik, warm relief washing over his body. They landed back on the log once more. Everywhere they looked, Tremidious' band of feathered fiends were in disarray. Battered, scattered, picked off one by one, half a dozen owls were already whimpering in submission on the woodland floor beneath them. Though the sight should have both gladdened and relieved them the feeling did not last long. Oswald looked over his shoulder, a cold sickly dread flooding over him like cold seawater flowing into his stomach. Tremidious had found them. He had no time to do anything but duck.

This last-ditch effort undoubtedly saved his life, for the cruel, scalpel like swiping claws of his attacker missed the neck they were aiming at. Instead, Tremidious' trailing claw ripped against the surface of Oswald's left eye, bursting it like a grape. The fluid from the ruptured organ started spilling down his shocked face like warm berry juice.

Instinct told him to propel himself upwards once more. He screamed down to Vik, "I have lost my eye! I have only got one eye!" His flight, usually so smooth and effortless, was ungainly and disjointed; a shocked, stumbling attempt at flight. The searing waves of intense pain lapping over him.

"Keep going, keep going!" screamed Vik, for he could see Javelin following in Tremidious' wake, having managed to escape the attacking trio of crows. His sharp owl's features were contorted into a mask of hateful vengeance. Oswald began to sob, the great surges of pain getting worse, as if that were possible.

"Vik I can't see, I can hardly see" whimpered the owl. Knowing now that it was all down to him to revitalise his flagging friend, Vik roared up at him in false bravado.

"I will be your eyes. Listen to me, fly as fast as you can, through that gap in the bushes over there. We can still make it Oswald, I promise!" The injured owl obeyed. He was near to giving up, but on hearing his pal's spirited commands, subconsciously decided to give it one more try. The gap in the sprawling mass of bushes that had colonised the woodland floor was rushing to meet them. Instead of getting larger as they neared it, it appeared to be getting smaller.

"Close your eyes," shrieked Vik, as they burst through the dark sanctuary. This only lasted a few seconds before they ejected out on the other side of the undergrowth. The air rushing past them cooled Oswald's burning wound. He felt slightly better.

"Have we made it? Have we lost them?" he inquired of Vik, without looking back. Vik swivelled his head around, opposite to the direction of which they were flying. His heart leaping into his mouth, his voice rising in high pitch panic.

"No! Fly faster Oswald, for all you're worth, they are nearly upon us!" Less than a metre away now, Tremidious, with Javelin following, had not been shaken off by the do or die manoeuvre. They had risked everything in the high speed implode into the tangle of bushes, as they pursued their quarry with grim determination.

As if struck by a bolt of lightning, Oswald recalled his earlier plan. If he'd been released by the two arresting owls that had held him securely on the forest floor, for a few frantic seconds he would have redoubled his efforts to escape. He would now put his plan into practice.

He frantically surged forward, wings beating so hard and so fast that Vik, slung underneath, feared they would tear from his body. This last-ditch effort drew out another vital gap from the villainous pursuers, when, all of a sudden, Oswald stopped flying, the life, the fire, seemingly to vanish from him. The height and distance they had gained would now be lost, the lifeless owl slowly spiralling down to earth with Vik screaming, then crying piteously as their end rushed up to meet them.

Behind them, Tremidious instantly detected his chance. His first bungled attempt at beheading

Oswald had not worked. He would not fail this time. He quickly turned his head.

"Stand clear, they are mine!" he barked at his Lieutenant. Immediately, Javelin winged away, watching from a distance with a savage longing to play his part in the stricken owl's demise. Able to close in on the fallen owl with ease, Tremidious had decided on a spectacular mid-air disembowelling. Blood and viscera would spray, rainbow like, through the air in a glorious, burgundy red curtain.

Almost upon them now, he opened his talons for the final strike and then twist, to shred flesh and feather. Then, in a millisecond, when he was only inches away from his quarry, Oswald jerked out of the way, as if yanked by a wire.

Tremidious felt an impact. A sharp pain, a few seconds of disorientation, his heartbeat rising in unison with his stricken panic. *Thump, thump, thump*, banged the overworked organ of his heart. He could see that he had impaled himself on a broken beech branch. Only small in diameter, but it had penetrated deeply, the blood red fluid of life pouring out of him like monsoon rain. Out of the corner of his eye, he could see Javelin, beset by half a dozen determined crows, his loyal lieutenant slowly succumbing to the mallet-like ferocious pecks. Tremidious, for the first time in his cruel life, knew what it was like to be afraid. No. Terrified. He flapped his once powerful wings twice, then he was done. His large head fell forward, his sabre like beak opening for the final time as he stared forward in now sightless oblivion. He was dead. Defeated.

Almost as if connected to him, his demoralised disciples fled. Sensing his death was the final breaking point. Never again would these owls band together to be the slave-makers of the sky. From now on, they would only kill to feed themselves, never just for sport, or pleasure. Exhausted, Oswald lay on his back, staring at the skies, beyond the treetops of the forest.

"You did it!" shouted Vik, with an air of mighty relief and triumph. Too tired to speak, and with his now empty, bloodied eye socket giving him plenty of pain, Oswald passed out. His ruse had worked. Tremidious, impatient as ever, had taken the bait that Oswald was beaten. Completely focused on their demise, Tremidious hadn't realised his peril until he impaled himself upon it with deathly force the moment Oswald had jinked out of the way. There was no escape for the king of the owls.

Oswald, now sleeping the sleep of the completely spent, could not hear as his little friend went on.

"Mind, I did play my part. I was great! When we get home, you'll have to back me up and tell all my family how brave I was. And it was me who came up with all the best ideas." He paused for a moment, remembering the attack of the two adders, and the near disaster inside the greenhouse. His appreciation of himself subsided somewhat. "Ok, ok, not all the ideas. But most of them." Vik stopped his excited ramblings. A look of joy and surprise dawned across his small, furry face.

"Oxy, Oxy, you are alive! How are you feeling?" There, scurrying to meet him despite his injured leg was his cousin, who apart from his leg looked to be in flush of health, quite buoyant despite his ordeal and imprisonment at the dark chasm.

"I am going to have my leg splinted by one of the crows. Says I'll be as good as new in a few weeks because of my fast metabolism."

Giving Oxy no chance to speak or explain, Vik erupted into speech. "You should have seen me! Cor, I was so brave. There was this one time..." Vik stopped his chatter. "Who's that with you?" Coming up from the shadow of a small sapling was none other than...

"Its you, its you!" Flapping his wings in a display of appreciation at this warm greeting was Caruthers.

"Nice to see you again old boy!" chirped in the crow, sounding as always very upper-crust. He went on, "Didn't think I would ever see you again old man."

"We thought you were dead, blasted by that boom pole the human was holding." said Vik.

"Oh don't you worry about me old Chap." said Caruthers. The crow went on to explain about how he had just managed to dodge the deadly blast of shotgun pellets. Pretending to be wounded, the crow had flapped off awkwardly in the opposite direction, hopefully making himself an easier target while Vik and Oswald got away. He was a gallant crow indeed. Then, when a few vital metres had been pulled out, he had dived down below the hedge bordering the field, giving the wood-be-hunter no target to aim at.

"Flew off to find the rest of the gang and tell them about our adventure. Anyway, it was no big deal, not for the first time I have had one of those things aimed at me," related the likable and confident crow. "Was not sure if you bought it or not. Then yesterday my nephew Carstairs told me how he heard all the commotion coming from far off, in the direction of the dark chasm. I just knew it had to be you lot. He should not have been anywhere near the damn place. Told him it was very dangerous, but, well, you know youngsters these days. Then when we got the hot news from an old racing pigeon friend that the dastardly lot were after you, well, called all the chaps to arms and we set off after you, quick as we could. Never liked that bunch anyway. All that damned hooting in the middle of the night."

"Well, as I was about to say, this strange black bird woke me up, knew my name, and led me over to you." Oxy interrupted at last. "Couldn't get a word in edgeways. Told me his name was Caruthers." the little vole went on. "No wonder we weren't attacked by the crows."

"Happy to help." answered Caruthers. "Right, we will give you a lift then. Getting dark soon, we have to roost for the night. Plenty to talk about after today's excitement." said Caruthers, eyes bright.

Chapter Twelve: A Place to Belong

He awoke with a start. Where was he? He turned over. He had slept on a luxurious bed of fur, leaves and grass. He felt refreshed, revitalised. He had no idea how long he had slumbered. His empty eye socket ached no longer.

A voice said, "I dressed that wound for you myself. I am Vik's father, Vernon. I would like to thank you on behalf of all the voles that live in this wood. What you have done is something that is both brave and remarkable. If you feel up to it, come outside. We have prepared a banquet for you. We are so very grateful."

"My name-" he was cut short by the senior vole.

"I know who you are my friend. Plenty of time for talk later. You must be famished." Oswald was indeed famished. He could not remember when he and Vik had last eaten. Vik! Where was Vik?

As if reading his puzzled look, Vernon answered, "He is outside. Come." He hopped out from under the tree trunk, squinting his one eye until it became accustomed to the light. In front of him was the most magnificent array of fruits and berries he had ever seen. It was indeed a banquet.

"Surprise!" Bursting out from underneath the covering of leaves were Oxy and Vik, swiftly followed by dozens of voles that lived in this happy community. To Oswald, it was a fantastic feeling to be surrounded by genuine friends, no matter what their size, no matter what they looked like. The younger voles scampered up his legs and onto his back and folded wings in wondrous fascination, giggling with delight. Oswald knew he had found himself, his niche. Here he was among true friends, who would take him for what he was. Never again would he have to worry about not fitting in, about being rejected.

The party went on until evening, the voles staying out late, more confident now with their owl protector in their midst. "Time for bed," commanded Vernon, in a kind and patient tone. The voles trooped back into the shelter of the fallen oak.

"Will you join us?" asked Vernon with concern.

"No. I will sleep in the branches up above. Could not get used to sleeping on the ground all the time."

"Ok. Take Vik with you for company." Oswald was about to protest, to quickly say that he would be fine on his own. But he could not refuse the warmth in the old vole's eyes. Nothing for it. Have to take Vik with him up into the trees. Oswald felt happy. He knew he would have another sleepless night while the little vole fidgeted and farted under his wings, but no matter.

Unfortunately for him, he had not banked on the return of the lovelorn courting dog-fox. His yowls of invitation to mate were even louder and more prolonged than a few nights previous. Again, with a groan, he braced himself for the powerful smell as the fox prepared to dung against the tree he had chosen for his roost once more.

The End

Printed in Great Britain
by Amazon

77107215R00078